The Draft-Busts

By
Jaime Guzman

This is a work of fiction. Characters, businesses, places, designs, events, locales, teams, names, and incidents are either the products of the author's imagination or used in a fictitious manner. Any resemblance to actual persons, living or dead, or actual events or actual organizations is purely coincidental.

E-book ISBN: 978-1-7367506-0-5
Paperback ISBN: 978-1-7367506-1-2
Hardcover ISBN: 978-1-7367506-2-9

The Draft-Busts 1
By Jaime Guzman 1
Chapter 1 5
Chapter 2 9
Chapter 3 13
Chapter 4 18
Chapter 5 23
Chapter 6 27
Chapter 7 31
Chapter 8 41
Chapter 9 48
Chapter 10 55
Chapter 11 59
Chapter 12 67
Chapter 13 71
Chapter 14 73
Chapter 15 75
Chapter 16 78
Chapter 17 86
Chapter 18 89
Chapter 19 96
Chapter 20 99

Chapter 21 103
Chapter 22 106
Chapter 23 109
Chapter 24 117
Chapter 25 127
Chapter 26 132
Chapter 27 136
Chapter 28 140
Chapter 29 143
Chapter 30 146
Chapter 31 152
Chapter 32 156
About Jaime 161
Acknowledgements 162

Chapter 1

Among the dying embers of baseball, I step back onto the mound for my last time. The coarse leather ball swallows the moisture from the calluses below my right middle and index fingers. My metal cleat tips are rejected from the top of the iron rubber. The small hole on the edge of the top digs deeper as my foot pivots in. My left knee rises and falls from my ribs just as my arms part away. Shoulders turn towards and away from home and I grunt in pain one more time. The ball flies.

This is the last time I am going to do this. The last time I will ever be able to do this. All the stress. All the arm pain. All the stomach pain. All over. Baseball is about to be over. Nothing left but memories of games that were forgotten the next day and right after the last game. Every single thought and practice of baseball won't be needed after this.

The bat tangs the baseball behind home. The red seams dance as they fly over the bleachers where my parents are sitting. They've come to almost every single one of our baseball games. Dad closed the shop and Mom took hours off from the police station to come watch me and my brother play. They were the only parents who came to watch every time. Sometimes, they were the only people watching at all.

The batter steps out of the batter's box and takes a moment to roll his shoulders and breathe. He's almost certainly going to be the last batter I face. Maybe the shorter kid in the on-deck circle might be the last one. But the nervous bony freshmen is going to be the last batter this senior will ever face. I've faced so many before since I started playing more than ten years ago. The last time I play baseball ends with us having a bases empty two run lead against a freshman who had to cover for a varsity illness. I get a new old ball and get ready to do it again.

Change-up No. Curveball No. Curveball No. Curveball No! Fastball Yes. Go through the motion one more time. Electric current bites my elbow. Foul ball. Hot air exits out between clenched teeth. Not again. I shake my arm loose as I wait for the umpire to give the ball to my catcher.

Sean gets out from the crouch and motions for a time-out as he trots towards me. The beginnings of the infield dirt kick onto the emerald grass. His catcher equipment still clunking loudly every stride he takes.

“Guy’s starting to get nervous out there. Give’m your curve. He’ll scare right off and the season’s over,” he says as he pulls off his mask and covers his mouth with his glove.

I cover the side of my elbow with my glove as I take a step off the rubber.

“Can’t we just go again?” I ask right before he gets to the mound.

“Keep it down,” he double taps his face with his mitt and I hide my lips with my glove. My elbow is still being bitten by a dog, “your curve breaks like crazy, he’s never seen it. Start off at his chest and it will break right over the plate for a strike. He’ll jump right out of the box when he thinks he’s taking one to the ribs.”

Sean grabs my shoulder with his mask and turns me around, “we should go for the fastball or change-up. I might get him out in front.” I look out towards the outfield and see past the chain link fence to the houses across the street. My sister's sitting in the front of our house watching the game from our front yard. She came back from the west to see me graduate in two days.

“He’s gotten way better contact on that last one than the one before. Throw a fastball again and he’s got a hit. You’ve never gassed anyone. You’re too short for getting past seventy. He won’t hit it if he won’t swing. He’ll foul off a change-up. I want to see that curve loop one last time.”

I exhale deeply and sigh, “one last time then. Let’s get one last strikeout.” One last strikeout. Haven’t had one today. I can’t let the last strikeout I got in my career be from a few days ago on a bunt.

He pulls me in a little closer with his mitt, “thanks for letting me catch you for the past year. It was fun being back there when you were pitching. I hope we get a freshmen that has a curve like yours next year. Shame it’s the last time I see something like that.” He flicks the ball into my hand and taps my glove with his mitt before clanking back behind home plate.

He crouches back down. Looks like I got a curveball to throw. I should have put a heating pad on my arm before the game. I figured they keep me in for a few innings then let maybe José finish up the game. He’s graduating too but he’s sat on the bench the entire last game of high school. What a way to end it all. I need a better ending.

I take one step off and look at the field for my last time here. The lime grass in the outfield. Our cement dugout. The clay dirt at shortstop where I turned two so many times when I wasn't pitching. I am a good pitcher and fielder but I don't have the physicality to make it past high school. Baseball is really meant for the guys who can make the big power moves. Balls in the outfield and fastballs hotter than flame. My brother's got the size and height to make it big professionally. If he makes contact that ball can go far. Too bad he can't hit anything and sucks at fielding.

I snap the ball up from my hip to my chest. At least my fingers don't have pain. Some guys throw the forkball and that can get some strikeouts but also a lot of finger pain. I won't have to worry about that anymore. After this it's just making money working with my dad at his shop. Everyday. Scraping by. I start getting a throbbing pain but I don't think it's from my arm. I have a pitch to throw. It's time to go through the motion the last time.

My left foot steps back then pivots with my hips as I stare right at the heart of the batter. It will break. My left leg surges forward as my right arm goes down and up making an L before I see it in front of me. My hand pops like a fishing rod and the ball rocket spins off of my fingers. One last jab into my forearm from the spin of the ball as it says goodbye.

The batter steps away from the plate towards third base and closes his eyes in fear. He swings the bat hoping to defend himself. The ball is breaking at least fifteen inches before it gets halfway to the plate. And so it ends in a strikeout. I guess I could take that as an ending. I had the best curveball out there and it's going to waste. But at least I got one last strikeout.

The bat starts to move and extend as the batter's left hand lets go with the right barely hanging on. The curve starts to fall off the horizon as the bat further gets closer to soaring away. The bat dips without the support of the left hand.

Dink. A slow roller towards Aaron at first base. The bat barely tipped the ball. Please brother, just let me get this one. Aaron sprints towards the ball as I follow through towards the catcher. I jet myself out of the motion and towards the ball. Aaron signals with his first base mitt that he's got this one and picks the ball up with his left hand.

I'll cover first base then, get set to take the throw and run along the side of the baseline. We practiced for an hour just for this play. Aaron motions to take it himself, ending all that, and shrugs off me and my second basemen whose also ready to take the catch. He trots and touches the bag with more than two seconds to spare.

The first base umpire raises his fist in an L shape and the game is over. That's it then. Aaron taps the glove of my second basemen and rolls the ball back to the mound. I'm never going to be on there again. I start to walk back towards the dugout as the rest of the team jogs back in. All the double plays and I don't get a high five from my second baseman. I don't need to clean up the mound anymore, no more good games at the end of this. It ended with a slow roller to my brother that I should have gotten.

"It was supposed to be more meaningful than that," I mumble to myself as I pass the gate into the dugout. It was supposed to be so much more meaningful than how it ended just now.

Chapter 2

I juggle the customer and the telescope as the paint dries and the radio continues to blare. The bottom shelf counter bumps forward as my weight fully presses down. Binoculars brush away as my right elbow pinches just before my upper arm.

"We can replace the signs as soon as you give us the designs you want us to make," I say into the receiver pressed on my neck. The viewfinder section is just out of my grasp as I step off the ledge before it breaks.

The older man on the end of the phone reiterates one more time, "we don't want them replaced because they were broken, we want them back because they were stolen. I don't even remember the designs we sent you." I can't reach the telescope even while standing on the lip. Why did my dad have to put the expensive stuff on the top shelf?

I take a deep breath as I move toward the back of the store, "we know your signs were stolen and that's terrible, but we can't return stolen signs to you because they were stolen. We don't have them here." The safety pins from the ladder screech one after the other just as the rock song stops playing.

The one hundred pound ladder grates past the back counter to the showcase of the store, each inch of movement scraping the floor. "Good morning Charisma City. We interrupt the music to let you know about one of our city's own, Jason Niagara." My elbow starts to tighten as I start to set up the ladder.

The voice over the phone gets more desperate, "but we need 'em back though. How will people see the sign for our new flavors if the sign's inside someone's bedroom?" I wonder what someone would actually do with a marketing sign? Interior decorating with marketing materials might be the new way to design your home.

I look back towards the counter and the drying paint on signs next to the register, "I remember helping design that sign especially the swirls on the vanilla ice cream. We may have that design on our computer still." One of four holes locked into place.

The female co-host cuts into the radio, "the professional baseball draft continues on and he's one of our best and made it in the second round." He's probably some godlike six foot three inch strong man. "This six four titan will surely succeed in professional baseball and we wish him well." A full foot taller than me, why am I not surprised? "Batting three eighty in his senior year at-"

"I think it was the ice cream parlor across the street that stole them. Can you go and get them back for me?" Huh? The ice cream parlor, their competition, stole them? If they stole them and get away with stealing, then the other ice cream parlor suffers since no one knows they have their product.

"I can't go and try getting your signs back. I don't even know where they are. How do you even know they took them? We can get you new ones if you want."

"But my store is losing money because they stole my signs. How can we get our message to the people that need to see them if they are just getting seen by some thief after they go out the door?" Reminds me of how when people were at second base they would try and relay signs to the hitter. It rarely worked because they would just change the signs after they got stolen.

"I don't even know who stole them there, but someone definitely did." But what if they didn't know they were being stolen? The hitter would know every pitch that was coming. Someone could dominate baseball if they knew exactly what the pitcher was going to throw, where it was supposed to be. Batting three eighty, they would be batting eight thirty.

The male host reads off the script of the news, "he is receiving a signing bonus of five million dollars." That's more money than almost everyone will make in a lifetime. It's more money than I will ever make here. But maybe my brother might make it professionally. I was always too short to play baseball, or any sport in college or professionally, I'm lucky to hit five four on a good day. Even though anyone can play any sport, all sports have the ideal body type to play. If you want to be a jockey you have to be very small. Basketball depending on the position, you want to be tall and thin, or big and tall. At first glance baseball isn't like that, when you look again the bigger, and taller you are, the easier it is to hit homeruns and to throw gas. More gas more strikeouts, more homers more wins.

"Can you tell us exactly what a signing bonus is?" the female sportscaster asks feigning ignorance for the listener. I wish they wouldn't do that, they know what they are talking about and should show that they know.

The last of the holes is set on the ladder, "give me a second sir, I'll check to see if we can remake the signs here." The dust on the top of the shelf sticks to the edge of my fingers as older spotting scopes get moved to the lower shelf. Some of the visualizers are actually antiques, but my dad still has them for customers that want to still be traditional signal readers.

The thousand dollar telescope to ship out reflects messages behind me, "it's a little complicated but they do it because they want to disincentivize him from doing anything else. It means that regardless of how well or how bad he does, so long as he finishes his three year contract he will get five million dollars."

"So he can be terrible and still get a bonus?" A laugh track erupts over the question, but a spark ignites as I look along the reflection of the telescope.

He doesn't need to actually be good at all to get money. They just need to sign him. And they signed him based on how well he did in high school against people who probably weren't very good! Jason might not actually be good. Aaron doesn't need to be good at all!

The first step down the ladder jabs a sharp pain in my right elbow as the telescope starts to slip out of my fingers. The box double flips out of my right hand as my left tries to grasp at its picture. My right hand flails and barely clutches the end of the pack. It tilts three feet along the ground.

I slowly try to lift the box back to the ladder as I feel my elbow tendon start to tighten. The string in my arm starts to strain and I wince trying to move slowly, keeping my balance on everything that is going on. As my wrist turns to rest the box on four fingers, the end of my forearm says that really hurts and let's go. I bite my lip so the customer doesn't hear me in pain.

"Don't listen to the bad mojo about you Jason, we know you'll do well. And yes all he needs to do is make it through the three year contract. But everyone else you just need to keep listening to the radio." I look down at the open box with glass shattered all over the carpet. The telescope in the box has been shattered and I'm going to have to repair it. But once something is broken it really can't be the same. You can try and hide the repair or work around the damage, but it's not the same.

"I'm gonna have to call you back something just got broken here."

"But my signs are being stolen and people are spending money across the street. They are spending it at the place that stole the signs. I even think the kid did it on purpose. There are twenty people there now."

"If you don't hear back in an hour, call back. If it's not me, tell my dad to call John." I look at the mess on the ground before seeing that the paint isn't dry yet.

Chapter 3

The eyepiece glares the November late harvest sun back towards my face. Objective lenses sit on the folding table looking back at me as the wind blows by. The soft cloth stops them from running away as I adjust the mount of the telescope.

Each adjustment moves me a little closer towards seeing home plate from home. The rebuilt telescope tube reflects the setting sun back onto me, inside the tube are a few modifications to realize new potential. The best is the one that brings the spyglass to the modern age from the age of wooden ships. A module that sees what the telescope sees and sends it to any attached computer.

One click on the eyepiece and I can see the gymnasium of my old school, another click puts me towards the baseball bleachers, one more puts me at the backstop. A click more puts me towards the mound but I can't see if this will work from here. The settings have to be perfect to be able to actually see the catcher, but there is no one there right now. I won't be on that mound again.

But that is what happens, the sport is over for me. As much as many kids see themselves or want to seem themselves in professional sports, no matter how hard we work towards it, it's probably ending before we get there. But that doesn't mean that it's not going to happen for everything someone tries their hardest at, just for sports. There are some things that can be taught but there are others that just can't be learned with athletics. Someone could train to become the best computer programmer in the world regardless of their physical body. But sports require you to train your body which has limits based on many things outside your control, that often can't be changed, like height and arm length.

My parent's car turns the corner towards our house. Aaron as usual has taken the front passenger seat from my mom. Even with the extra leg room Aaron still looks squished inside the sports car.

Aaron has the chance with the body type that he has. From his six foot four inch height to his ability to explosively move anything under two hundred pounds, he could have made it in most other sports except maybe being a jockey. His shorter dark hair may have been a detriment to wrestling, perhaps his shear bulkiness makes a difference on the track team, broad shoulders filled with muscle that he hardly had to work to get. Yet we both only played baseball, it's all we ever did.

My dad slowly coasts the car as it pulls into the driveway. Parking brake applied and everyone gets out of the car. Aaron and my mom start to grab groceries from out of the trunk as my dad starts to walk towards me.

"Have you fixed the telescope yet?" my dad asks as the lawn grass brushes away.

"Almost, part of the tube had to be glued together and I had to add an electronic module."

"That's making it not an antique anymore John. No one is going to buy it with that part on it," he says as I look at the other options on the table. Let's see how this one works.

"It was sitting there since I was six, if someone wanted it the way it was they would have bought it a long time ago."

My dad takes a look at the black module and the telescope aimed at the field, "you know baseball is over right?"

"I know I know, I'm just testing the distance ranges for the lenses and I'm going to check for clarity." The empty baseball field unkept for the football season has weeds in the outfield and an ocean along the five six hole.

Aaron runs back from outside our home, the edge of his pants grazing the corner of the bush beside the driveway. "Aaron could you run over to home plate and throw some signals like Sean would do?"

"Baseball's over," my dad shakes his head as he turns towards the car to get groceries.

"I just want to see the depth of field, Aaron run over there give me a signal." Aaron looks towards the groceries and sighs before taking a jogging pace out of our driveway onto the concrete. His legs hold and control his one hundred eighty-five pound frame perfectly as he starts to judge the outfield fence. Hardly breaking stride, he grips the edge of the fence and flies right over into center field. He continues running through the outfield.

"Well you can keep trying to get back on the field but you won't be able to. We all have a time with stuff we love, but then we move on to make money." But this could make a lot of money. More than I will ever see doing anything else.

Aaron crosses into the infield, kicking the dirt up with his shoe as he passes second base. Aaron always had the strength to throw a baseball far. He could probably send one over here from second base. I haven't thrown a ball since May, I'd probably be lucky to make it across the street. My right elbow pinches as I swivel the telescope.

I look through the eyepiece and Aaron starts to come into focus. The back of his jacket fully covers the view of the telescope as he runs over the mound. Empty bleachers blur in the view where I'll be watching his games in the spring. Depth of field range for this lens is quite small but the good thing is that a catcher can move left and right but not forward and backward.

Aaron gets to home plate as he starts to cool down from the brief run. He pulls out his cell phone and I hear a ring on my phone.

"Ok, so can you see me good? How does the telescope work?"

I put the phone on its speaker as I lay it on the table, "I have you in focus right now." I start to turn the knob on the eyepiece. "Take a step right behind home plate." Just make sure this is the setting I'll use.

"Put up some fingers for me, give me a fastball outside then a curveball low and in."

Aaron takes a catcher's stance and signals one wag to the left then two fingers brushing down. It's perfect! I rocket out from the telescope and give a thumbs up. The rolling of rubber wheels turns the corner.

"John you got the depth?" If I can see it in the telescope it will appear on my computer and it will go to my phone. I will see exactly what the pitcher and catcher are saying. What they are thinking. What they are going to do. I'll be right in their head and so will Aaron.

Ping. Ping. Ping. A orange sheet goes between me and Aaron. White paint stops me from seeing the field.

What! A car is blocking the way! It's the neighbor, he's blocking the way! Move! Move!Move!

My neighbor shakes his head at me as he steps off the running board with his lunch pail. He isn't going to repark his truck. His work truck with ladders, equipment, and cargo laughs at me with the forty feet of empty space in front of it.

"Aaron get back here, All I can see now is a car window," I sigh towards the speaker.

"I'll walk over to the dugout to get out of the way. Do you need to check any other lenses?" he asks as he starts to get into a slow jogging pace.

If a car is parked in the way then I wouldn't be able to see the catcher during the games. I need a clear line from my front yard to home to see the signs. But this only works for home games, how am I going to do this when Aaron plays at another school?

The neighbor clicks his alarm to beep, "no it's fine I think I got what I need."

Aaron starts to jog back to the house as the telescope mount gets put away. Without the telescope it's a little hard to see fingers from here, but even if I would, I couldn't give them to Aaron all the way from our front yard.

Our phones disconnect as my phone goes into my pocket. Slowly I move the telescope back into our house. What once was useless and a waste is now something that is so powerful, that no one out there will be able to stop it. This deserves to be repainted from the bronze glow it has to something new. Right now it will go right by the window looking towards the field. That's what it's going to stare at for sometime.

Groceries are starting to be put away and I should probably start helping Mom. I reflexively grab an apple and toss it in the air with my right arm, a slight pull on my lower forearm and just as reflexively my left hand grasps the apple before it falls to the floor. That should be that last time that happens.

"Hey Mom can you get some traffic cones from work and bring them here? I only need two," I ask as I grab some carrots with my left hand and place them in the refrigerator.

"I might be able to get some from the city public works. What would you need them for John?" my mom says as she finishes looking through a work folder. Sometimes she brings her work home with her, and the stress.

My bottom teeth graze the top of my lip, "I'm hoping to help Aaron practice parallel parking in front of the house. It's better he hit a traffic cone than our car or the neighbor's."

She grabs some food from the grocery bags and puts it in the cabinet, "your dad should really be the one teaching him that."

"You're right but it's still better that he hit some cones from your work than a car, or something else. He could even use them as a baseball tee."

She begrudgingly takes the bait, "fine" she says, just as Aaron jogs back into the house.

Chapter 4

Set pitch order to curveball low and away then fastball inside, slider inside. Repeat. Pitcher type righty. Begin. The avatar of a shorter pitcher glows into the screen. He gets into a motion and the animation of the ball turns into a real one just as his hand passes the black space on the screen.

The ball starts to dive half way from the plate. Tilting slightly towards Aaron as he lowers his bat into a swing. He tightens the swing just as the ball gets to the plate. Slicing down with the thirty-three inch bat, the ball dives just below the end of the barrel. The padding behind the plate thuds. Another miss.

"These machines throw too fast for me to know what's coming John. Can you lower the speed a bit?"

"Only one or two kids are going to throw at this speed. Everyone else is throwing faster than this." The pitcher goes into his windup, the leg kicks and the ball streaks on the inside corner. Aaron shortens his swing as the bat handle rubs against his waist. Thud on the padding.

"Well that's why I miss, you know we don't have much time to know what pitches are thrown. By the time I know what it is, it's already in the catcher's mitt." One more thud as Aaron takes a step back towards the batting cage door. "You want a turn?"

"No there would be no point, I'm not playing anymore." One more bang against the padding before the pitches stop. "We are going again."

Aaron sighs as he steps up to the plate one more time and sets himself up. I set the pitcher to a lefty with a change-up curveball mix. If he can't even hit the ball with my help then there is no way this will ever work. I'll have to reassemble the entire telescope and I'll be watching baseball from far away until I can't see it anymore. Those people who make millions of dollars just out of reach.

"Fastball up and away," I sigh as the pitcher starts his motion.

Aaron's gaze is aimed right at the pitcher. His arms start to lower just as the ball leaves the machine. His already large toned biceps bulge as the bat starts to whip across the plate. The ball squeezes just as it touches the bat before going straight back towards the screen. For the first time I hear a tang as the ball hits the other side of the cage.

I hop up and down unable to contain my excitement, "Yes! Now curveball low and away!"

The pitcher oblivious to me telling Aaron the signs continues to go through his animation. Aaron sets himself up again, waits patiently with a smooth swing; drives the ball straight back at the screen. A real pitcher if they saw what Aaron could do would be very nervous to pitch to him.

"Fastball up and in!" This will work! Aaron sits back on the fastball before firing the baseball on a line towards the back. Aaron takes a deep breath in as he resets.

"I'm going to up the speed and break on the pitches," I start to hear the machine rumble its engines louder and louder. That won't do anything to Aaron.

"I'm gonna start missing," Aaron shouts as his eyes are hyper focused on the pitcher.

"You won't! I'm telling you each pitch he's gonna throw and where. The next one is about ninety-four miles an hour low and away get ready cause it's gonna be fast."

Aaron relaxes his shoulders as he prepares for the pitch. Almost eighteen now. His wider eagle-like eyes and square rock jaw relaxly focused on the pitching machine.

The pitcher reaches down the mound and the ball rockets towards the outside edge of the plate just above the knee cap. Aaron's swing, what once was multiple jerks as he tried to touch the ball has become a single motion with the force of his one hundred eighty-five pounds. I could only find the ball after it had already sped past the pitcher.

I need the radar gun! Where can I find one? I look around the batting cage area nothing, past batting cages and towards pitching booths. They might have one there. Slightly used baseball bats adorn the walls ready for use. I pass the payment booth of the batting cage as the young technician looks at what me and Aaron are doing. The booth full of gum, tokens, and sports drinks doesn't smell like a dugout but they do their best to make it look like one.

"Just keep hitting Aaron. I'll be right back," I shout as I walk pass baseball bats for sale.

"Great back to missing again," Aaron sighs as his swing goes back to a step, collapse, and a lunge.

I run towards the pitching mounds passing the last part of the batting cages where younger children are learning to swing a bat on a tee. I remember vaguely hitting off a tee when I was younger. One of the tees plops to the ground after a five year old hits the middle of it. One day if things turn out right for you, you might be able to get paid to hit a baseball.

I hear the snapping of mitts from the multiple catchers who are here. Occasionally you can pay an employee to catch for you but most of the time you typically bring someone to be your catcher. Though there was a few times when a few kids would show up to catch to get some practice in. Almost a dozen mounds of different types, some with a sand dirt, others with a clay and others more of a hard board more often used for tournaments.

Aaron actually had an offer when he was fourteen to join a travel baseball tournament team. He had just finished his growth spurt and people obviously started to notice this huge kid walking around. They figured cause he's so big he has power and can block a lot at third base even though he's a lefty. So he tried out and most of the balls got by him at third base so they moved him to first where there's less action, but he wasn't able to scoop most balls in the dirt even if he was way taller to get high throws. They booted him off the team after the second tournament when they realized he can't hit.

More popping sounds as I pass behind the nets behind the catchers towards a wall of radar guns. Some slightly dirty radar guns mount the walls for use to see how fast a pitcher throws each of their pitches. I look at the descriptions on each one make sure that I can read the speed past one hundred miles an hour. If the ball is coming in at more than ninety, then it has to be going back even faster than that, maybe faster than one hundred, one twenty even.

Good to sixty miles an hour. Nope. Up to one fifty with a five mile an hour margin of error. No that's too much. Former police radar gun, decommissioned this is perfect to borrow."

"Mind if I test it out?" I yell back to the technician at the entrance of the mound area.

"Which mound you planning on using it on?"

"Not the mound, I want to test at the batting cage."

"Those machines are accurate to plus or minus two miles," he says as he waves me over to the payment stands.

“You don’t have to worry about our machines we calibrate them weekly and have a staff member-”

“I want to see how hard my brother’s hitting a baseball.”

“That’s a first. You want to see what the speed is of the ball speeding off of the bat.” He starts typing in his computer. “Hmm, I’m supposed to charge people for using them on the mounds. Use it at most for five minutes, and drop it off at the batting cage check in station.” He takes a glance at the batting cages. "Let me know how fast it is,” he asks as he starts to tug at his faux umpire shirt.

I nod to the technician as I walk away once again from the baseball mound. My right arm is glad that it doesn’t have to throw again. The snapping of the mitt shifts to the tangs of baseball bats and the thud of the mats behind the hitters. As I slowly get closer to Aaron I hear a constant pattern of thuds. Thud. Thud. Thud.

“Alright Aaron, we are going to reset the pitcher. I’m gonna see how hard the ball is coming off the bat. I’m gonna tell you exactly what it is and where it’s going. Ok?”

Aaron still hasn’t taken his eye off the ball as he keeps just trying to make contact. The pitcher finishes his motion before freezing in the set position. Turn on the radar gun. Set the pitcher as a righty sidearmer with a fastball and cutter, set pitch order to three of each, all in a row. All outside for a lefty.

“Swing the best you can Aaron, we got this. The first one is a fastball on the outside part of the plate.” Aaron looks back at me just as I push the button to go.

Aaron’s front leg briefly goes towards his hip and rockets back to its spot pivoting as it hits the ground. His hips jolt around as the bat struggles to keep up. His shoulders just slightly big for his shirt, most shirts, stay coordinated as they dip towards the plate and ball. His arms extend beyond his core and the outside of the plate. I lose the ball as it hits the bat picking it up right after it gets to the pitcher. One hundred and fifteen miles per hour.

Same pitch same spot. One hundred and eighteen miles per hour. Last fast ball at the spot. One hundred and twenty-two miles per hour. Cutter outside part of the plate. Swing and a miss. Aaron’s swing deteriorating as he chopped on the pitch. “It's coming at that exact spot again Aaron. Same exact way." A perfect clash of metal and leather. One hundred and twenty-six miles per hour.

Last pitch before we quit. Aaron who once couldn't react to the pitch, now knows what is coming. The nerves and anxiety of wondering where and what pitch it is, are gone. Aaron leans his weight slightly on his backfoot, then shifts as his cleat lands right on the edge of the batter's box. Swinging slightly upward the bat comes a long for the ride as it collides with the ball sending it towards what would be left field. One hundred and thirty miles an hour.

My jaw drops, "Aaron we are done for today." Aaron rolls his shoulders as the pitcher disappears off the screen.

He opens the door and walks outside the cage, "good I think I might have cracked this bat." One last grip before he hands it off to me.

"You swung so hard that you cracked the bat!" That shouldn't really be possible. Well it's going to be time to look for a new bat. "That last swing would have been a homerun in any baseball park. It came off the bat faster than I ever seen before, at that angle that would have landed over any fence you'd ever play at."

"Yeah too bad I can't do this in a game," he chuckles as he returns the bat to the booth.

I place the radar gun on the counter and wave to the technician by the pitching mounds, "who knows Aaron maybe this season will be your year."

"In that case I'll need a bat, better than that one."

As we walk out of the sporting goods store I see just slightly behind the manager's window. A gleaming baseball bat. Along the wall, a solid never used bat with the letters ICU on it.

Chapter 5

My hand touches the knob just as my hand starts to sweat. I'll wait until tomorrow. My hand recoils back from the door. I've been putting off talking to Aaron about this for too long. I wanted to tell him what I wanted to do since the beginning. But Aaron might not want to do this. What if he tells mom? We could get in big trouble for doing this. We've played baseball together since the brief moment when I was taller than him, but this isn't really playing baseball anymore. I slowly turn the knob. This is the moment where it either happens or it doesn't. I don't want anyone else to hear what we're talking about.

Aaron never put much baseball stuff inside his room. Most of the stuff on his walls are different styles and types of glass. A few glass cups that he blew with my dad in the back of the store when he was younger. A hand held telescope that dad gave us from the store after he first opened it up. A runner-up award from the eighth grade science fair.

"Did you like mom's pumpkin pie?" Aaron asks as he keeps looking through the microscope on his desk. They gave him a biology assignment over the Thanksgiving break to write a report on certain things he sees under a microscope.

"I did," I sit down on the edge of the bed. "It tasted really nice." The November air chills the room. Across from me the open closet with a few practice jerseys, a few pairs of shoes that are now too small for Aaron. After he passed me up when he was nine I started wearing the clothes that he couldn't fit into. All the newer stuff had to go to him because he was outgrowing it all the time. Always in his shadow, always left behind.

"I actually helped her make it, secret ingredient I put in was some ginger."

"That's why it was so tangy," I readjust myself on the bed. Let's go through with it, "Aaron do you have a second?" I stroke the edges of my short black hair back with both hands.

He scoots away from the microscope and swivels the chair, "What do you need John?"

I sigh as I try to find the right words to say, and how do I even say them, "I want to help you play better baseball." No immediate rejection from Aaron. This should be way easier, I've thought this through a bunch but now getting someone else on board with this. It's no longer an idea but something real.

"Of course you do, why else did you pay for me to hit at the batting cages for the last few weeks?" he chuckles as he quickly turns the light off the microscope.

I jolt as I state the obvious, "but you know you really can't hit the ball if you don't know what's coming. You're way more likely to bat one hundred than two hundred next year. I've spent how many years playing in the same infield as you, you gave me so many errors on the balls I threw, and you're gonna give whoever is taking over shortstop a heart attack every time you have to scoop."

"Duh, it's hard to hit a baseball and they pay people that can actually do it, millions of dollars to do it. People like Jason, and not people like me."

"You can hit the ball if you know what's coming." I lean towards Aaron across the bed, "I saw you inside the batting cages."

"I think anyone can hit a pitch if they knew what was coming."

I go blunt, "I can have you know what pitch is coming every single time."

Aaron wants to ask if I know how to read minds and if I could teach him. That could help him solve lots of problems. I wish I could do that, but this is the only other way I can read a mind right now. I can't read the mind of a math test but I can see the signals on a baseball field.

Just push through, "our house is right behind center field. You know that telescope that I've been fixing? I can use that to give you every signal that every catcher is giving and they won't even know. You can only dream of how well you'll do. You'll win a banner for the school." I slap my hand against the bed before I snap my fingers, "have the greatest hitting season of your life."

He smirks, "so you're gonna be a cheerleader in front of our house jumping up and down fastball change-up."

I start to present my main idea, "you know how our teammates would shout 'get a hit now kid, get a base hit now kid, you got this Aaron?' Well, I will say those things while you are up to the plate, but depending on what the pitcher is going to throw, I will say something in particular. Maybe for a curveball low and away, 'make some solid contact Aaron.'

Fastball up and in 'go Aaron.' You can hear me from home plate from the bleachers if you just listen for me. I'll blend in right with the cheering that fans and players say."

Aaron adjusts himself inside his leather seat he got for his birthday last year, "so, you're not going to be signaling from our house, but sitting on the bleachers behind home?"

I start to rub my knuckles with my fingers, the calluses fading away from pitching, "I changed the telescope that I broke to transmit what it sees to a computer, that computer will give it to my phone. That telescope in our front yard is gonna be aimed right at every catcher. They won't even have a clue with the codes I'm saying. You can become the dream baseball player with the signs I relay to you."

Aaron puts his hands over his face and breathes loudly into them, "baseball isn't my dream, John. It's yours." His arms cross as his hands come off his face, "you love this sport more than I ever have. If someone called you to play I think you would be off in a minute. We would basically be cheating. But let's pretend I did do that and then they put me in professional baseball for the rest of my life. I don't want to do that, you do."

I continue pleading Aaron, "I'm not asking for your whole life, I'm just asking for two years, well two and a half. They don't sign any players for more than two years at most three when they start, but they give big bonuses to convince you to spend your time away from everything else."

"What happens when high school ends, and we can't cheat anymore? Our house doesn't move to every outfield we play at."

The one thing that I have planned out. "Then you are labeled a draft-bust and after your two years in professional baseball you retire and go play with microscopes. No one would ever know, they would just think you couldn't transition out of high school baseball. But you got the millions of dollars from the signing bonus."

"You're lucky I'm not telling mom you want to cheat," Aaron slides back toward the microscope and turns it on.

I get off the bed and move towards the desk, "well do it for mom and dad then." I shut off the lights to the scope and it goes black. "You know how many people would love to have the capability you have. So many people would trade everything they had just for your physical body to play a sport. You spend a few moments of your life and never have to worry again. You have no clue how hard it is out there in the real world trying to get money. What if something happens to one of our parents and there's no money to pay for it. Even the slightest of disasters cost money to deal with and they happen to a whole lot of families. What happens if mom loses her job or dad gets sued and we have no money. That's why! That's why we need to cheat. For the money." Aaron glares up at me and I take a few steps back.

"Aaron if you don't want to do this, then I will just put the telescope back on the store shelf and I won't ask you this again." I start to motion slightly to the door, careful not to make him upset.

"We do this one thing, and then you don't get me involved in any of your schemes again."

"Ok. If you don't want to talk to me after all of this. I get it. But this will work."

Chapter 6

The third day of winter conditioning was even colder than the first two. Thankfully it hasn't snowed in Charisma City in over one hundred years. I stare towards first base as I continue mowing the front lawn. The baseball team's first games start in late January so the team starts to practice in the middle of December during the winter break. Have to get practice in, especially warming up pitcher's arms.

My right arm pinches just as I start to turn the lawnmower back towards the front of the house. My dad gave me some tasks to do around the house while he worked on a couple things at the store. Mowing the lawn is the last one. It's more noisy than anything but at least I can see how Aaron is doing at practice. They've shifted from warmups to taking grounders in the infield. Someone else a little bit smaller than Aaron is standing right beside him taking turns with Aaron at first base. Two lefties at first base.

Two more passes over the lawn to be complete. A ground ball right along the line of first base. The six one kid lunges towards the ball and gets it just by the end of the glove. He springs back up and fires back to the catcher at home. Aaron's turn and a high chopper between him and the second baseman. Aaron makes a dash towards the ball, stretches and barely misses it. Markie my second baseman easily curves the route to the ball. Picking it up on a slide he's ready to fire it at first base. He double pumps and waits for Aaron or the pitcher to get to the base. A fast runner would have been safe. I know the coach noticed that.

The final pass along the lawn before I'm done. The clear cut of the grass reminds me of how the infield used to smell at the start of the season. I fill the small hole right in front of the lawn mower making sure it won't go off-balance as I pass. Thankfully now we can play baseball inside a dome. Or at least professionals can.

The third basemen each take grounders and on purpose are throwing the ball bad. A hop before the base. High above base. Aaron, simply by being big, could make up for the scoops that he missed. Simply reaching up from his height gave fielders a lot more room for vertical mistakes. But now someone else is there. Almost as big as him.

I slowly roll the lawnmower back into the garage and pass by the two traffic cones my mom lent me and our garbage bins. These are the perfect way to ensure that no one is blocking my view to home plate. Put the garbage cans along the curb of our house. Place the traffic cones right across the street making it impossible to park along the viewpoint. Remove as soon as game is done to ensure that no one complains or notices.

The tryouts for the varsity baseball team continue on with everyone hoping to make the team. I walk towards the front of the house and see some of the junior varsity kids doing sprints along the outfield fence. Sometimes kids will sit on the bench for a year and wait on a senior to graduate to take their spot. They aren't good enough to start, but they have one more year than the varsity player does. That player graduates and then the other guy takes the spot. All without having to personally improve at baseball at all. I see Eric who was my backup last year have shortstop all to himself.

The coach calls the first basemen to take batting practice as a screen shaped like an L is brought over to the pitching mound. A smaller screen is getting placed behind home plate as the catchers are called towards the bullpen on the left of the field. Please don't let this guy hit good.

A first attempt at a bunt and it is a miss. Second attempt and it is right back towards the pitcher. Good but first baseman typically don't bunt anyways. The third but first real pitch slings right back towards the L shaped screen. Well he can hit. The next one he pulls right down the right field line. The next a grounder between short and third. Just don't be too good. Give me a chance with my telescope.

Bang as he hits a fly ball almost going out of the park towards center.

"Head's up Head's up!" I hear Randy my backup centerfielder shout as he sprints towards very deep center.

Most of the kids running near the warning track look up and try to cover their heads. The centerfielder gives as much of a chase as he can. The ball losing gas before it gets to the fence. It's not gonna be a home run. Thank goodness that would have ended it right there.

The ball hits just a few feet from the warning track and bounces high. The ball spins against the plastic shielding on top of the chain link fence and crawls right outside it.

"Hey John toss the ball back here." At least Randy remembers me. The JV kids continue on with their exercises towards left field and the bullpens.

"Randy why can't you hop the fence and get it?"

"With these cleats I'll hurt myself hoping this. You played infield, you've never twisted your ankle hoping a fence." I continue watching the kid hit balls all over the field. The other center fielders taking turns chasing the balls that are being sent across the outfield.

"You don't have cleats on anymore, just run over here and get me the ball back."

I start to walk across the concrete towards the baseball field. The last of the Autumn leaves have fallen off the trees as winter is in its peak. I've heard that in places that play inside of domes they can climate control different parts of the field for the players. I would have loved to play in those once. Being able to play at shortstop where it was eighty degrees while you have no clue of the temperature outside.

"Whose that guy playing first base?" I scoop the ball in with my left hand and toss it just up a few inches then back down again.

"Seriously, John?" he watches me toss it one more time in the air. "His name's Zack, I think he moved here at the start of the year. Looks like he's taking over your brother's spot. Now come on give it."

"Well tell coach that Aaron always doesn't do well in batting practice. Wait for the first game." I toss the ball just over the fence and Randy grabs it with his barehand and fires it back.

"Coach is gonna probably have Aaron be sitting on the bench the entire season the way this kid is hitting. I could probably take a nap in the outfield when he's up to bat," he says as he turns around and runs back to compete for his spot on the field.

The batter uncurls his neck as he gives Aaron a spot to hit. Please just make some good contact. All the time in the batting cage had to be worth something. You can't be that bad.

Aaron this time taking batting practice no help from me. I really couldn't help if I wanted to. How am I supposed to know what pitch that guy behind the screen is throwing? There isn't a catcher there.

The first pitch and the bunt goes straight up into the air. That would have been an easy out by even the catcher. The second pitch and Aaron bunts it right between the hole of the pitcher and third baseman. Ok that's not as bad.

Third pitch swing and a miss. Just keep your eye on the ball. Swing and a miss. Swing and a miss. Come on Aaron it's batting practice, can't you just make any contact? The first piece of contact from Aaron sends a foul ball towards the dugout. A faint chang against the fence as it duds to the ground. Just hit the ball fair. Ground ball to the shortstop. This is going so bad Aaron. I can't vouch for you anymore.

More swings and misses off pitches that I can tell from here move just slightly. Of course the pitcher is gently mixing it up. But even a minimum variety is too much for Aaron. Just tell him what you're gonna throw and he can hit it. Bang a sharp ground ball right to the second baseman. That's the best hit so far.

The batting coach raises his pitching arm in the air signaling the last pitch. Was that enough of a hint for what he's throwing? Why didn't I set up the telescope to see?! The ball leaves the coach's right hand as Aaron winds back for the swing. The bat flies at the ball and the ball shoots up into the air between right and center. It's out of the infield but it's not going to make it over the fence. It won't even make the outfielders take a step back.

The right fielder shakes off Randy and parks himself beneath the ball and takes the catch just outside the range of the second baseman. Randy shakes his head at me as he runs back to chat with the other people he's fighting for center with.

Even though I'm in my driveway I can see Aaron staring straight at me and then back at the other first baseman and shakes his head.

Chapter 7

My parents and I pass through the front gates of my old high school as we walk to see Aaron's first game. Right after the school bell rings, we go by dozens of high schoolers leaving from the brisk January cold. I recognize a couple of them as they walk towards the parking lot. A wave towards one guy that sat behind me in math class last year and wave again towards him. He looks at me confused and then waves back wondering who I was.

"I'll be right over there, just give me a chance to see something," I say as we pass by the gym on the way towards the baseball field.

I dart inside the gym to see if it's still there. I pull open the glass door into the foyer of the basketball gym. The squeaking of shoes against the floor echoes even past the doors. Aaron said the basketball season playoffs are ending tomorrow and any basketball-baseball players are going back full-time onto the field the day after. Today is the final practice for someone inside there. I hope that their last game is as exciting as they need it to be.

I open the next door into the gym and see a few of the very tall varsity players taking three point free point shots in the beginning minutes of practice. Some of them are even taller than Aaron. Aaron would be about average height with most of these people. The coach whistles to them to hustle into a practice play. A few kids staying after school, either because they're bored or because they have nowhere else to go relax on the bleachers. One glares at me wondering what I am still doing around the school after I graduated.

John Base was here please still be there. John Base still be there please. I take the steps on the visitor side bleachers towards the second to the top row near the edge. In my senior year me and Aaron would go and watch some of the games from that spot. After a while of watching the games on the wrong side, I got dared to carve my name into the bleachers. Even after the basketball season ended and we were at the baseball field, I'd go there every week to make sure that it wasn't filled in.

It's not there. It's not there. Where my name was has been filled in with an adhesive filler. Finished over with a new gloss over the bench. There is no evidence that I was ever in attendance. I didn't win a banner. Most people I recognized earlier don't remember me after a few months. In less than a year I've been forgotten at this school. I sit down and look around at the walls of the gym. I never got a banner here. This was the time in my life where I had the most ability to really do anything and I don't even have my name on the bench anymore. The basketballs keep going towards the net some missing, some getting right in the net. I take in a breath of the ugly air, it's ugly and smells like old wood, feet and sweat, but it was mine for a little while. I get up out of the seat.

The wooden bleachers clap each step that I take down the stairs. I guess that's it then.

"When they call blue dog they are throwing the ball to their small forward two seconds after he touches the paint," the sixteen year old girl says into her phone.

Sitting with a blue cap over her long brown hair, she is pointing her phone at a wide view of the court. From basically anywhere here she could record a practice. She is recording the practice for someone. It's for the other team in the playoffs. Who else could it be for?

"You didn't see anything did you?" she asks nervous about getting caught. What would happen if I got caught doing what I did?

I remember that they called special plays roughly ten percent of the time. If they got the ball in the game roughly seventy times that means seven plays. If the other team stopped half of them that's four plays roughly six points off the game. Maybe the other team gets four or five points from the rebounds off the unexpected blocks. That could win a game. She starts breathing heavily as she stares at me.

"Stealing the play calls? Watching what the plays are? That be crazy. All I saw was some weird girl talking about dogs," I say as she collapses back into the bleacher seat. She blows her lips together as she lets out the biggest exhale.

It wouldn't make sense on doing this on every single game. But on the games that matter, you might have to take every single advantage that you can get to win. I wouldn't be surprised if professionally they are going to try that.

The last steps down the staircase are even heavier than going up. The last time I'll ever come inside here. Aaron will be out of this school in May and I will have no reason to be here. My cousins don't live around here so I won't see this place again for anyone else playing.

I open the door to the entrance of the gym and see the gleam of the trophies before I exit the front. I guess those don't matter to the people who had those, they went on to do things that make those trophies look small. They have all let go of those trophies eventually and got new ones. But I guess that's why some people hold on to the trophies they have, because they aren't getting any new ones.

I check my phone right before I make it to the bleachers where my parents are sitting. The camera is working perfectly. Set in focus from the last few days. So long as the telescope is in the right spot it will work every single time. I can see my telescope and laptop set in the front of the house. No one is going to steal it especially since there are people across the street that would see them. Set up in the middle of a neighborhood even kids walking home aren't going to touch it.

Phone battery full, laptop charged. Ready to go for the first time. Deep breath as I sit on the green painted bleachers next to my mom and dad.

"I think you left the garbage cans out," my mom says as I start to stretch my legs on the plastic seat.

"You also left the telescope out there. What's taking so long with that anyways, it still can't be broken?"

I can't muster the strength to figure out what to say and just look at the field about to have players on it.

The baselines lined with white chalk, the grass cut, the coaches talking to the umpire, just about ready to do this. I see Aaron just from the end of the dugout waving at us, me to get over there.

I point to myself before I rise out of the seat and start to saunter over towards Aaron.

"When you get there make sure you give Aaron some water I brought," my mom says as she hands me a bottle of water.

Mom always loved watching us play. She would have been worried sick if either of us played another sport that had more physical contact. Baseball thankfully doesn't have that much contact. With the exception of the catcher on foul tips, the only real potential contact is when you pitch and the ball comes back at you which is rare but could happen, and at first base with a runner running into you after he hits the ball.

The takeout slide at second was taken away when I was twelve. Running into the catcher has been banned for twenty years. My mom always told me that she wants her kids to be safe. Well with this I think I can keep Aaron safe long after the last out of the season.

I go to the left side of the dugout, I lean past the green bricks and over the hip height chain link fence. This fence is the only one that doesn't have a plastic covering on it. Would make running up against it and reaching over for a foul a lot easier to do. Less painful.

Aaron speaks to me from the edge of the dugout corner, "I'm batting last. But I still have first base for now. Sean was talking about how Zack might get the call to pinch-hit and then take over first depending on if I don't do well today."

"Take it easy, don't worry I'm right there watching the catcher all day. Just focus on getting the ball at first base and take a hit from the ball if you have to stop it from going by you."

Bluntly he says, "you know that hurts right?"

I blow my hair up, "yeah I know it hurts I've gotten hit in the chest with a comebacker before, lucky I didn't break a rib there but yeah, if I can take a hit at my size your size can take a hit." He looks nervous as he grabs a baseball for warming up the infield, "just remember what we went over. I know the pitcher. He has a two seam fastball, slider, sinker, and a change-up. Only focus on what I am saying. I am going to be extra loud." Aaron runs out towards first base. Running around the pitcher's mound as the other infielders are glaring at him. They are wondering what took so long.

I walk back towards the bleachers and pass the makeshift concession stand set up by the baseball parent league organization. At least they are getting some money for baseball programs from people who show up.

"He's batting ninth today," I say as I sit back down.

"Weren't you taking him to the cages for weeks?"

"Yeah, but there are some good kids out there. He might move up if he can do well today."

Aaron throws a ground ball to the third baseman. The third baseman double pumps and glides around the pitcher's mound and releases the ball into the grass in front of Aaron. Aaron stabs at it and misses.

Please don't throw any bad throws people. "Come on defense strong throws out there."

Sean calls for balls in and they are ready to start the game. I look at my screen and I see Sean give the signals to our pitcher. If I can see Sean I can see everyone. Save the battery for Aaron. Line drive towards the shortstop quickly caught and back in to the pitcher. Please don't make Aaron have to do anything. First base already doesn't have to do much, but there are some things they have to do. The cut off man for throws to home from the right and center fielder. Holding runners on base, not to mention dealing with bunts and actually coordinating with the pitcher on them.

More batters and thankfully nothing going on for Aaron. They go back into the dugout and I look back towards the telescope, still working just waiting. The home team gets its at-bats but I don't care what happens only Aaron. I look at my phone and start figuring out the signs. One fastball, duh, two change-up, three slider, that must mean the sinker is number four. Easy when they don't even know. Visitor's out at bat again. Base hit and Aaron holding the runner. Don't throw a low pickoff towards him. Flyout strikeout walk. Groundout to second to the shortstop. Second time up for the home team. Aaron would be up in four batters. Make that the next inning now, nothing happening. Two flyouts and a strikeout. Now Aaron is up to the plate starting off the inning.

Let's go. Phone is on and I see the first signal fastball low away.

"Pay attention your brother's up to the plate." I am paying attention Dad. Way more than anyone could ever think.

"Get a hit now Aaron!" Mom shouts.

"Make some solid contact now!" I yell at Aaron. Fastball away.

Aaron takes the first pitch. About six inches outside. Good take. Need to have better counts. Hitters do better when there are more balls in a pitching count and pitchers do better when there are more strikes. Once you're at two strikes you only need to get one more to get an out. Once you're at three balls you only need one more to get a free base. As you get closer to either or both outcomes the at-bat tilts towards either the hitter or the pitcher.

"Make some solid contact now." Same exact pitch. This time for a strike.

The catcher positions himself on the inside part of the plate, change of pace.

"Free swinging now kid!" my voice getting slightly masked by the kids in the dugout saying the exact same thing. No one has a clue.

The pitcher goes into the windup, his leg kicks up then down towards the plate as he drags his back foot slowing his momentum. Aaron revs and makes hard contact with the ball with the front of the bat. Skyrocketing along the right field white chalk line foul. The right fielder running towards it then stops as it tilts just out of the field of play. The center fielder signals to his troops back back back. He can hit it far if he makes contact. He's big. Don't let it turn into a triple what could be a double.

I see the pitcher rub his right hand over his face just as he gets the ball back. Be careful with this kid. Change-up no fastball no slider yes outside backdoor.

"Drive it the other way Aaron," I relay. Thanks telescope.

Aaron takes his stride towards third base as the ball comes in. Just a little low on the pitch and the ball flies way up in the infield. The pitcher points up as he gets off the mound. The catcher takes off his mask and searches for the ball way up in the air. He finds it and calls off the third baseman running in. Caught right inside of foul territory. The catcher throws it around the horn as I see the pitcher take off his hat and wipe away the sweat on his face. He won't have to face him for a while. Don't worry I've got more ready next time.

"Keep your eyes off your phone. You just missed your brother almost get a double."

Back and forth as time goes by, hits strikeouts, Aaron slowly is getting back into the lineup. Fifth Inning with only two left to go in the game we get another chance.

A runner on first base and one out. Aaron hasn't made an error on first base today but he needs to get some action with his hitting.

"Get a hit now Aaron" I shout, sinker inside low. Ball one. Fastball outside as they are trying to play safe as possible. Two balls. Ok this is a good count. The pitcher checks the runner on first, he wants to keep him close. An extra few feet might mean a run if Aaron gets the ball in the outfield. He is going to get a double right here. Change-up inside now.

"Free swinging now kid." Aaron cocks back just as the pitcher releases the ball. Bang. I barely see the ball leave the bat as it zings towards the outfield. Then suddenly it's not. Leap and the first baseman gets it just on the edge of his glove coming down towards the ground. The runner on first jolted towards second stumbling as he tries to get back towards the base. First baseman pounces, runner dives. Double play. Inning over and they have to go back out. You got lucky pitcher. Aaron rips off his batting gloves as he walks towards the dugout and a benchwarmer gives him his mitt.

"Almost a double right there," my dad pushes my shoulder, "you completely missed it." They are going to get mad at me as this season goes on. The better he gets, the more it's gonna look like I don't care. But I care way more than either of them possibly know.

The sky starts to get dark as they turn on the lights to the infield and part of the outfield. The school was lucky to build them when this school was built over fifty years ago. Thankfully, as the winter turns to spring they will need these lights less and less. Down by three it's unlikely we'll have to be around here for extra innings.

Fully illuminated scoreboard turns on just along the left field line. Its right edge acting as the edge to the left field foul poll. Out of play to ensure that a ball that would hit it is a foul ball. They probably thought when they were placing the sign when they were building the school, because it's out of the field of play no balls would hit it. Not true, but at least if Aaron gets a homerun it won't try blocking it with its fifteen feet of height.

Aaron now in the hole in the seventh inning with one out. Someone just needs to get on base and Aaron gets one more chance. Waiting at the end of the dugout for his turn, he keeps his head down on the bat. I then see him wave his arm towards himself. He wants someone to go there. I bolt towards the dugout, the bleachers tang as the steps go by. Check my phone, the lights aren't bothering the telescope.

"He's probably just a bit anxious," I say as I push my way towards the end of the bleachers.

"He's due for a hit," my dad says as he starts to zip up his jacket. More than you think. He is going to get a lot more hits now.

A passed ball thuds against the soft padded backstop as the count begins. A timeout called by the opposing manager. Looks like they're getting a new pitcher. They decide to call in the right fielder to pitch just as I get to Aaron. Right, time to learn this guy's pitches. Need to talk to Aaron at the same time.

"You ready for this Aaron?" I ask just as the ball gets handed off to the closing pitcher. Lefty ready to close the game as best as he can.

Aaron's head's face down, "I don't think we should do this anymore. It's not working."

"You've only just started, you would have had two hits today, just got unlucky on both of them. One guy made a great leap, other one landed foul deep in the outfield." The pitcher pulls his glove towards him. Change-up. "This next one is almost certainly going to be a hit."

The pitcher curls his glove towards the plate. Curveball coming in, "if it is not I don't want to even try this anymore."

"Ok. If this doesn't work then, we'll do something else." I remember my name's spot being filled in. I brush my short strands of dark black hair away from my face. Fastball. "Just focus on the timing right now. Make some solid contact." Fastball curveball change-up that's all he has. Aaron's bound to remember the code words we set up.

The warmup is done and the batter steps back up to the plate. A fresh arm against two batters better start studying. May have another pitch. I have my eyes glued to my phone as I slowly make my way back towards the bleachers.

The temperature chills just as I get halfway up the bleacher steps. Groundball down the third base line. Third baseman dives toward the ball and gets it snugly in his glove. Push-up against the cold ground. Dirt covering his uniform. Throws with all his might towards first base. Out number two by half a step.

The team's new left fielder takes his turn at the plate no hits so far today. Good for Aaron maybe he can advance in the lineup next game if he gets a hit right now. Come on kid get a base hit. Aaron needs to go up again. Just one more at-bat. Ball one. Just make good contact. Two fingers down and the ball loops towards the dirt. Ball two. Don't swing. Ball Three. Don't you dare swing that bat. Ball four.

He trots to first base as Aaron takes his steps into the box, left-hander hitter facing a southpaw pitcher. The odds should be against Aaron but they are not.

Two fingers down and the catcher shifts his stance towards the right.

"Wait for your pitch if you have to Aaron," I shout, eyes glaring at the screen. My eyes dart up from my phone and the curve lands just inside. Strike one. Ok Aaron won't just be standing there today. Change-up outside. "Let's go Aaron," I belt out, the yelling after each pitch scrapes the back of my throat.

A little low. All equal at one. One finger down swishes it away from Aaron, the catcher semi-squats up. Fastball outside but it's up this is the best pitch he's gonna get.

"Gotta take command out there Aaron!"

The pitcher darts his eyes one last time at first base and right back at the plate. High leg kick and the ball leaves his hand. All down to this single moment. Aaron's arms stretch out as his feet stop just on the edge of the batter's box line. One pitch to determine it all. Bang!

The ball booms towards center left field. My eyes go away from the screen. Outfielders giving chase. My parents rise up out of their seats and cheer. Jumping inside the dugout. The two outfielders give chase but they won't get it, it's going too fast. Ball starting to lose just enough steam that it can't be out of here but it's going way into deep left center. Way deep. The runner on first base rounding second. The ball bounces fifteen feet before the wall before touching and going right back towards the center fielder. Cut off throw and the runner is held up at third base. Aaron trots right into second base.

My parents cheering for Aaron as his face lights up. But I don't think it's from the night lights. He looks around at how he is at second base for the first time in a long time.

Aaron gives me a thumbs up. We got it. This is going to work. The pitcher gets the ball back from the shortstop and looks at the mess he got himself into. Runner on second and third. Two outs and the start of the lineup again.

That ball he just hit could have gone much farther with a better bat. We need one, much better than that one he just used. That bat made the ball lose speed when it should have been a homerun. When they start hitting homeruns. And a lot of them the scouts notice in an instant. The harder and farther the ball goes, the more likely that we get extra base hits. Show he has power with his batting average.

If we get a better bat that turns singles to doubles, doubles to homeruns. We haven't had a homerun here since I was a freshman. Now I think Aaron might just get forty this season.

Chapter 8

Fourth bat so far. Eighteen swings in. Not optimum. I look towards Aaron and signal to try the next one. The bright lights of the batting cage hide the fact that it is near closing time and most of the people here have gone home. Even the mound area which I remember always having someone doesn't have anyone there right now as those lights go out.

"We're going until they kick us out," I say as he regrips the next bat with his fingers. Should I tell him to use batting gloves? Maybe it could improve his grip. It would release some sting on balls that get hit on the inner part of the bat. If it is a colder night game he could be able to get a better grip. When I pitched and it was cold the bat just drained the heat from my hands and I couldn't control the bat handle. If Aaron loses a little bit of bat control, then it means less hits even with the help I'm giving him.

I run towards the batting cage check-in station, "keep going Aaron." They may have some batting gloves there or else we're going to have to stop and search for them and see what they have.

"I think I'll just wait till you get back," he says as he steps to the side of the batting cage leaning against the side tarp as pitches go by.

The check-in station, has semi-healthy snacks, helmets and older used baseball bats for anyone to use. Some people have given their bats to the batting cage after they couldn't play anymore, others traded in used bats for bats at the cage they really liked. There was one time that a person actually cracked a bat that was being used in the middle of hitting. Sprayed the entire front of the batting cages with composite material.

"Got any batting gloves to test out?" I ask leaning over the managed corrugated green iron counter running towards the back. The back television talking about sports news and how Jason Niagara is doing well. Aaron's name might just be on there soon. Whose Jason Niagara?

Starting to seal up the equipment, the mid-twenties worker responds, "we have a couple if you want to borrow, but everyone has been using them, you'd probably want new ones if you plan to actually use them in a game. See how they feel brand new."

"Can I take a look? My brother's hands are bigger than mine but he needs to see what gives them the best grip." Jason Niagara looks to be getting a sponsorship deal. That's more money too. Would have to work extra fast on that. Professional athletes have to do other things for their league besides play, they have to do goodwill activities to promote themselves and the teams to the public, they have to get sponsors for advertising. As much as I don't want to think about it, sports are as much image based as ability based. If people don't like the sports team or there are no sponsors then there is no money and no team. Athletes have to spend so much time on that, almost as much as practicing.

"Take a look at these three, these would probably fit him. You might want to have him get over here to actually try them." The technician pulls a few pairs of still attached batting gloves from their hooks and spreads them on the lukewarm green iron. The first pair has some extra padding on its palm, the material feels too slick to be able to grip the bat well. I would love the second pair. Material feels like it has extra grip and is extra sturdy. Third pair has more padding than the others on parts of the fingers, that could help with shock on a poorly hit ball. But Aaron is only going to be making good contact."

The blond haired technician waves my brother over to the stall, his tired eyes droop as he continues preparing to close up.

"If you're looking to improve hitting you're going to need a great bat. Gloves will help but a bat will do so much more." The blond technician picks up the phone underneath the desk and calls the manager. I wonder if on slow days he takes a couple swings inside the batting cage. I haven't taken swings in a long time, I think if I swing a bunch without a good bat it might damage my elbow even more. The shock from a pitch right near the handle can rattle your hands for hours. Have to make sure that Aaron doesn't hurt himself with any bat we find.

Walking with a slight limp as he turns the corner from his office, the manager says, "you can go home if you want, I'll take over. I'll give you the commission for this one. I'll close up." The slightly portly early forties manager just has the start of grey hair on the edge of his mustache. He looks behind the counter to take a look at the bats still there. Everything in place as the technician leaves towards the employee section. "Now, I've seen you inside the batting cages here almost every other day. Do you think you can be a professional baseball player?"

"Oh yes definitely," I gush out.

"Wasn't asking you. Asking your brother there," he says as he takes a look at the baseball bat we have been using. Deep in thought, his mind races, he brushes his short brown hair away from his face trying to figure out what to do.

"I don't know, maybe if some stuff happens."

"Hmm right on the edge of greatness, just missing one or two more things. I know what you mean." He looks down at his lower left shin and wiggles it. His khaki pants pretend to be baseball manager pants even though there is no team, just a few employees.

"I don't know if I'd make it far professionally though," Aaron says.

"Making it professionally even it is just for a brief second. Even if it doesn't last for more than a moment, is still making it. So many people get so close but never actually get there," he jars his leg. "I have something you might want to take a look at. Give me a sec. The bats in this store are good but I know a better one," he says as he turns around towards his office. Every few steps his left leg slightly buckles as he passes a row of baseball equipment.

"What do you think?" I ask Aaron.

"I'm only going for the minimum amount of time as a pro then I'm done."

I sigh, "I meant about the store manager guy."

"Looks like he's been injured for a while in his leg. I was learning in science class there are these tendons that can't repair if you get certain injuries. Long rehab even with surgery." Sports medicine, maybe I should look into that. No, then you're just nursing an athlete back to health after they injured themselves. You're not playing the game, you're not involved in it. All the drama, all the action, all play isn't there when you're the doctor. You'd probably hope your patient stopped playing so they didn't hurt themselves more.

He walks back with a black wooden glass case. The faux grass crinkles against his brown dress shoes as he gets toward us. The angle of the case just barely revealing the eyes of the bat looking out from the glass.

He unlocks the left latch on the case, "This scepter is the only one of two of its kind. Me and one of my best friends engineered this right as we were leaving college." The right latch unlocks as he sets the case down on the table. "This will beat any bat that is allowed today."

Thirty-four inches long big barrel. A dark blue knob before a thin but strong black wrapping. Minor indentations on the grip that are less than a millimeter deep provide extra grip to the bat handle. The noir tape extends just a tad shorter than other bats. Two inches after the tape, four small open eyes, each covering one part of the bat. Those eyes always see everything around it. The top and bottom of the open eye at first looks normal but really it is the ruby stitching of the seams of a baseball. From top to bottom all bright red stitching just misses its neighbor circling the eye but never touching. Pearl white eyeballs end next to a slightly above center alert red iris that never rests and always judges. Just inside the bottom of the iris a darker eggshell white center showing the aperture of the eye.

The bat case opens letting us see without glare the entirety of the bat in clear view. A dark blue coat just matching the knob from the end of the tape to the top of the bat. After the four eyes around the end of the handle; bat information just as the bat starts to go from thin to large. Weight in ounces, length in inches all in a whitish tint. A green row of olive leaves that really are another set of eyes mark the end of the bat width growth and then another row of eyes revolves around the bat just past that point. The same eyes all around. Across the barrel of the bat at a slight angle are the golden letters I.C.U. The sweet spot just between the C and the U. Closing out the top of the bat two inches before the end another set of eyes watching everything, then a blue-black top covering the true end of the bat.

"We were going to make a whole entire series of these bats, but then things got in the way. We designed this using the pinnacle of our chemistry, statistics, engineering, and physics knowledge to make the perfect bat. We looked at the bat regulations and this bat meets the regulations for every league we could find. Special technology to make the ball go higher and farther for better hitting outcomes."

Aaron grabs the solid well made one piece of hitting, "Why haven't you sold it yet?"

"It's the only one in existence. There is a thirty-three inch bat currently in the glass shelf of the head of the surgery center of Charisma City General Hospital. He kept the other one after we made it. If I sell this one, I will never see it again. It's always watching and judging those that are around it. I won't give it to someone who can't use it the way it should be used."

"Mind if I take a few swings with it?" Aaron says as he takes a slow hitting motion against an imaginary tee.

"Go ahead, let me change the balls coming out of the machine though," he says as he opens the door to the batting cage and walks towards the back door to the pitching machines, "real baseballs to show you how well we made this."

Aaron steps back into the batting cage as he likes the bat. Takes a few solid swings outside the batter's box before the machine starts to pitch. Perfect.

The machine starts to roar, "we added weight near the end of the bat to give it more capacity for power. A guy like you can easily manage the extra weight at the end. When you have just a little bit of end load on a bat it can add a statistically significant ball travel distance." The first pitch comes out and Aaron steps up into the batter's box.

The screen next to the door lists fifteen fastballs in a row low and away.

"Just make some solid contact out there all day Aaron."

A glorious sound from the bat as the ball flies straight back to the machine. Next pitch rockets back to where deep right would be. The ball jetting faster off the bat then ever before. If we weren't inside a cage that would be a homerun. More pitches more speed hitting the sweet spot of the bat with all the eyes watching the baseball. More Homeruns. Doubles. Triples. Runs batted in from the outfield. The last pitch flies towards the bat and the cover of the ball rips as it leaves the bat towards right-center.

The avatar of the pitcher disappears and the manager comes out from the back of the cage, "this bat was made by people who were in a crossroads of their life. They didn't know where they were going so they took one step in and some left, others took a step then another pivoting away from this while others stuck around."

"This bat is amazing," Aaron says as he smiles towards the bat.

The click of the ground reverberates as the manager walks back towards us, "I'm glad that someone can finally appreciate my work. We made it perfect."

He continues, "do you think you can hit as well as you did in here out in the game?"

"With this bat he will break records in high school and professionally," I remark.

"How much will it be?" I ask. This will be a lot, especially for a prized possession.

He pauses as he thinks hard, "five hundred eighty-four dollars and ninety-nine cents." He readjusts himself from what he says, starting to let go, "that was the amount we were going to sell the line of bats at. We designed the bat to be the best bat available. Most of the bat companies care about keeping the cost down, but we didn't care because the most important thing about a bat is how well it performs. It's the perfect bat and the cost reflects it. I promised him that if I would ever sell it, that would be the price. We might have gone lower over time with technology naturally decreasing production cost, maybe have gone with different materials if a league changed their baseball bat standards, but we calculated the exact price to create and keep making this work of art. If your brother uses it, it will finally get the use it deserves, not just sitting and watching me in my office."

That's a lot of money. How am I gonna pay for this? This bat is the best one there is and all that's stopping me from getting it is a little over five hundred dollars. I have some money but I will sell anything I need to get that bat for Aaron. He will be a superstar with the bat. So many people could be a superstar with it. And right now there is only one here.

I respond, "ok give me until tomorrow and I will get you the money."

He takes a moment to look at the bat and nods. He puts the bat back inside the case and walks towards his office as we start to walk out the building. What will I sell to get this bat? Aaron wouldn't sell anything but I will give everything I have for the bat. I see the manager look back at the case one last time saying goodbye in his head.

He jolts towards us, "oh wait. I'll throw in batting gloves that me and another friend made while we were looking into the baseball industry. On any bat especially after significant swinging without using batting gloves you have a higher chance of developing blisters which significantly dampen hitting ability. Just give me a second." He runs back into his office and I see him open a safe through the opaque window. Inside has store ledgers, money and gloves inside another case. Places the bat back on his desk as he grabs the gloves.

Coming back out from his office as we wait near the front of the store, he shows the gloves in the case. The baseball music and background cheering of a fake crowd echoing near the entrance. One day soon that crowd won't be fake.

"We actually made these batting gloves before I convinced my doctor friend to make the ICU with me. My surgeon friend actually didn't make these so, these gloves aren't actually affiliated with the ICU. Right after we made these, the guy I made these with decided he wanted to be a detective and left the baseball industry. He has a small detective agency in Steel Springs now."

On the front, black leather with extra padding on the thumb and index finger. Tiny small holes at the joints of the fingers to let oxygen in and sweat out. At the end of the wrist the same blue color as the bat. Hook and loop fastened gloves. Turn over the gloves and on the back right hand the letters C.U. and on the left the word LATER. No eyes on the back of the gloves but they still know that balls are going to go over the fence. The blue color takes over the entire glove except for the letters in gold.

"Perfect style choice too, even though these gloves aren't officially with the ICU make and model, still looks nice with it," he says as he puts the gloves back in the container. "He named his agency C.U. Later after the name we used for the gloves."

"The ICU bat always watching always judging," ready to purchase tomorrow, "I'll get you the money."

"I made a promise to them that I would give them half the money we made from anything I sold." Well I hope the doctor hears on the news that we are using his bat. Maybe he will hear it after completing a surgery.

Chapter 9

The first time I faced a flamethrower as a hitter I buckled down and hoped that I didn't get hit. He must have thrown at least ninety-two, this guy is throwing much harder than that. The just above six-five lanky lefty is throwing heat, if he can keep this up all day he might just be able to have a perfect game. Against most people.

Fastball with the natural cut of a lefty, change-up which really is just a slower fastball, curveball that has some movement but the fastball is what gets most of the work done. Sometimes when you throw so fast you don't even need to hit the corners and make it harder to hit. The speed itself makes it hard to get contact. The faster it goes the less and less time people can determine what pitch it is. If they can't figure out what pitch it is and it all looks the same, you're guessing where it is going to go.

You'll probably have to adjust your swing to be able to put the bat where the ball is. You have less time to react. Poorer contact or no contact. More strikeouts. It's easier to get that speed when you have height and longer arms from that height. You also get to scare most people that are shorter than you when you're on the mound. I only got to do that twice in my entire pitching career. The flamethrower I faced struck me out twice and got eleven more strikeouts that game.

Aaron's moved up from ninth in the lineup to seventh after the first game. The coach is skeptical if he can actually hit especially after poor practices and last year. But he is willing to take a chance that Aaron shines in the games. Or even the spotlight.

The eyes on Aaron's bat have their eyes on me as he stands in the on-deck circle. He has watched over that bat like crazy since I ran back to buy it. He practically yelled at Sean when he got near it. Everyone's been staying away from it since. Don't touch it. It's very important. I had to get rid of some old stuff in my room for the money to buy it but it was worth it for this bat. The first time this bat is going to be used in a game. The first time all the eyes are watching.

Two scouts are here for the opposing pitcher. With speed like that, so long as he can get somewhere in the strike zone he will make it, they just need to make sure. One looks like a college scout other professional. Need to do good today against this guy to make them see Aaron.

"Ninety-eight miles per hour. Two miles faster than the last pitch," the scout says as the other scout starts to write down. The older scout pulls out his flip phone and makes a call. Letting them know how well the rocket lefty is doing with four strikeouts in the game thus far. Make it five as a strikeout on four pitches. Aaron does well today he's moving up higher and higher.

Aaron walks up to the plate and takes his stance in the box. Feet barely farther than shoulder width apart. The bats eyes looking at the pitcher and right at me wondering what I see from the near top of the bleachers. Fastball away and up. "Gotta take command out there Aaron!"

"One hundred and one miles per hour." Aaron takes a step out of the box and blows an O out of his mouth. Strike one. Stay calm out there Aaron. It's scary but you're the only one that can do this, I can't do it anymore.

Thank goodness this is the only person in the league that I think that can do this. If everyone threw this fast, then this would just be striking everyone out all day. I faced this guy once before. He tried scaring me off the plate because since I'm so short I can't reach the outside part of the plate without stepping a little over the batter's box line. Almost nicked my jersey but I went straight back on the edge of the plate.

Fastball inside. "Give it your best hack out there Aaron!" I shout. My eyes dart towards the field. Strike two. The catcher rifles it straight back towards the pitcher. He's ready to throw it around the horn again. You have to swing the bat Aaron. I can give you the signs, but I can't swing the bat for you.

Curveball inside. "Wait for your pitch if you have to Aaron!"

"Don't listen to him Aaron two strikes mentality!" my mom shouts to Aaron as the eyes glare back at me. "Are you trying to have him strike out?" I lean my head down into my puffy blue jacket.

Boom! The sound of the all seeing eyes awakens everyone in the stands. No more no-hitter. The white patch of the ball goes way over the second baseman's head into the center field gap. No more waiting for something to happen. Aaron sprints as fast as his ox legs can take him. The right fielder sprints towards the outfield fence racing against Aaron to get the ball back to stop him. Rounds first base as the right fielder's almost there. Go Go Go! He's got it as the coach waves him to third base. Run

Run Run! Turns past second as the second baseman has the ball on the cutoff. Testing the arm Aaron slides into the base. Ball bounces into the third baseman's mitt. Safe.

Mom and dad cheering up and down. I rise up to high five my mom and dad. Aaron raises his hand as he calls for time.

One of the benchwarmers carefully carries the bat to the dugout and puts the bat right back in the corner spot that Aaron sits at, the eyes keep watching me wondering what I just did.

The pitcher takes a look at Aaron right before he takes the mound for his windup. Even though I stopped looking at the signs, I can still see that he's wondering how did he get a hit. What went wrong with that pitch? Is the kid this good? He is that good. The college scout writes stuff in his notebook.

Aaron gets stranded on third base and he goes out to first after putting his helmet and gloves away right in his spot. CU LATER. I still see them looking at me. The pitchers on our team are being switched out left and right as both sides haven't scored yet. More dominance by the flamethrower with hardly any of the speed going away after three more innings. Aaron is up again once again, They are both waiting on me again.

Curveball no. Fastball yes. Wiggle inside no. wiggle outside yes. "Make some solid contact now!" Next game we are going to have to sit closer my voice is starting to hurt. Ball one and he rifles it right back. Curveball inside. "Wait for your pitch if you have to Aaron!" I look back towards my mom who is glaring at me, "You have three more strikes to play with?" I mumble as I go and relook back at the screen. Strike one. Change-up no. Change-up no. Change-up no. Fine change-up inside. I signal to Aaron just before fireballer goes into the windup.

The blue edges of the bat glisten, the eyes gleam just as his bat starts to move. Aaron's front foot lifts and shifts towards right field. His body twists as the bat's eyes go through the zone and the eyes hit the ball. Kaboom! Way faster than the flamethrower can throw the ball sails towards deep right. Keep going Keep going. The right fielder giving chase. It might make it. It might make it!

The ball smashes against the top of the wall and sticks to the chain link fence. Right fielder throws his hands up in the air immediately. Aaron is now stuck at second base and this time much much closer to a homerun.

The pitcher walks to the catcher as the right fielder fights with the fence to get the ball out. Small dent in the fence. A millisecond difference and that would have been our first homerun. We may have one more shot today.

The two scouts are starting to talk to each other. The professional scout points towards Aaron and gives a fake swing. An inquisitive look from the other scout towards the dugout. Aaron Base. Why haven't we heard of him yet? Aaron Base. Why haven't we heard of him yet?

The pitcher and catcher go back to their places and Aaron takes his lead off of second base. Not giving any signals to anyone else. Small lead hoping someone will get a hit after him to bring him in. Bottom of the lineup not likely but who knows what can happen. Strikeout and another strikeout is what happens and inning over. Come on you have to give Aaron a chance at bat.

Sixth inning away one run scores. Sixth inning home still bringing in strikeouts with no sign of being tired. Pop-up infield. Pop up to the centerfielder to end the inning. Please don't bring in a closer to end this. Stay in there. We need another shot against this guy. Statistically, we are going to do great against him.

Seventh away. Reliever comes in and keeps the score one zero. Speedster in the other dugout is going crazy that he isn't getting run support and is carrying the team. Again. I know how that feels. Having to pitch your best and still have a close game because the other guys on the team can't get runs for you. Playing perfectly but having to deal with an error in the infield and having to pitch more and more. The coach blaming you for the run that came in that should have been stopped by good fielders.

Seventh home final at-bats. The scouts are getting their notebooks out after watching the game go by the last few innings. Four five and six haven't done much today, they are getting ready for Aaron. Four is up to the plate to start the half. Someone get on base need to give Aaron a chance.

"How long has he, Aaron, been on the team?" The scout with the goatee asks my dad.

"He's been on the team for all four years," my dad turns towards the scouts at the very top of the bleachers. "He's really improved on his hitting."

“I don’t know maybe you guys just haven’t noticed him,” I say.

My mom looks at me, “well you won’t notice if you’re not watching.” I put my head down again as Aaron waits to go on deck.

“That kid has excellent power,” the scout says to the other.

The other scout brushes him off, “I don’t know, we haven’t seen him before. I think that our guy can blow it past him to seal the game.” We will see about that. This game’s over once Aaron’s at the plate. He isn’t going to be looked over by scouts any more.

Strikeout. Eleventh one for almost seven full innings. He is responsible for more than half the outs in the game. Next batter. The six almost a half foot pitcher sees Aaron stand next to the chainlink fence by the dugout exit and realizes he needs these next batters out. If Aaron gets up with someone on there is a huge chance of him losing the game. Strike. Ball. Fastball ding. Grounder to the shortstop and the throw double skips across the infield grass and the first baseman misses it. Is Aaron on the field? Safe at first as the runner stays firmly at the base.

The pitcher glares at his shortstop right before he gets the ball back. I know that feeling of making a game costing error. Almost always the pitcher is the one upset with you the most. The most weight of the game in his arm, carrying that weight can do so much damage.

Number six up to the plate. Fastball in. Strike. Change-up away ground ball to the third baseman. Run Run Run! Don’t get thrown out at first on the double play. Throw to second overthrown as he tried to get it out as quick as possible. Runner sees it go into the outfield and runs to third base. Right fielder has it as he pockets it seeing he isn’t getting the runner at third. The pitcher is steaming mad at his defense. I know how you feel man.

Aaron up to the plate. This is it almost certainly the game. Catcher sets up outside. Change-up no Change-up no. Curveball no. Curveball fine. Sets up outside breaking away from Aaron.

He is setting it up for a ball. “Do your thing Aaron!” I shout as the few people in the crowd stand up. I rise up after realizing the people are standing without me.

Ball one. Close close. Almost a strike by mistake. Ball back to the pitcher and he is eyeballing the runner back to first. One finger down inside. “Give it your best hack out there Aaron!” Swing and a foul ball towards the visitor's dugout. Wake up call if anyone isn't wide awake at this moment in the game. He was just ahead of a hundred mile an hour fastball. Change-up no Change-up no. Change-up no. What is wrong with you, he mouths as he calls for a mound visit. Glove over mouth. Just the fastball only the fastball. Mad at the catcher for what pitches he's been calling and giving hits away. He gasses people so step on the gas. I have to do all the work myself. The catcher puts on his mask again before going back behind the plate.

Fastball outside. "Make some solid contact!" A little to much off the corner. A strike. That's a bad call. Don't be trying to make it up right now blue. Two strikes one ball.

The clicking of cleats from the home dugout as they give him support. Outfield respecting the hitter. Runner staying close. Fastball low and in. Yes finally. Checks the runner. Right leg lifts and the ball flies.

Boom! The perfect sound of the bat echos throughout the park. The ball skyrockets straight towards center field going going. No doubt about this one. No doubt about this one. Cheering erupts from the dugout as the ball sails over the center field fence. It's gone! Over the street and into our backyard. I think it's ours. It's either that or in the neighbor's behind us. Aaron trots around first base as the team runs out the dugout to home plate. That was the first homerun here in a long time and we're keeping that ball.

My parents are cheering for Aaron as they run off the bleachers and towards the backstop. Aaron trots towards home as the rest of the team welcomes him. I go towards the backstop just as I turn off my phone.

The game is over. The pitcher slams his hat and glove to the ground pissed off at his defense for not getting him out of the inning earlier. He walks back to the dugout pissed off that he lost after throwing a near masterpiece of a pitching performance. The score board in left shouts Three to One Charisma City. The excitement reverberates through the air as I watch the celebration of the team. I hear the clanking of the scout's shoes as they walk down the bleachers.

"If a kid like that can hit him, what do you think professional grown men could do against him?"

That's the wrong thing to be thinking now. Time for me to shine. I stop them just as they get down the bleachers. "You should be thinking this; if a kid like Aaron could hit like that against someone like your guy, imagine what he would do professionally."

Chapter 10

Tubulated and non-tubulated electrodes connected to the ends of the glass. Argon gas fills the warm tube. Heat the end of the tube to create a vacuum in the system as I separate the newly formed sign from the processing machine. The sign is almost complete.

Dad is talking with a customer in the front of the store as I start to roll the Faux Silver from one end of the sign to the other.

Even though it's called Neon signage, it actually can be a different type of gas depending on what you actually want. Argon gas makes things bluer while actual Neon gas is more of a warmer color. Then you have to have a set glass color to ensure that it's the color you want. Glass of one color plus gas of another equals something completely different. The glass really is green but it is showing a blueish tone with Argon gas.

It's actually very dangerous to be messing with signs like these if you don't know what you are doing, or are careless. Some Argon signs contain Mercury depending on the desired color of the sign. Faux Silver looks like Silver, but it really is very dangerous Mercury. You break open the sign and you get exposed to the corrupting nature of Mercury. Making you sick, contaminating everything around you, long term negative effects that you won't realize for a long time after you break open the problem.

Roll the ball over the loop, nothing drips out. If the sign is compromised by impurities from outside forces, like air from the outside world via a hole in the glass then it won't function properly. Only when it's pure can it be truly enjoyed, but yet it can be sometimes enjoyed better with the corruption of Mercury. That's why it's put in there despite how bad it is. If they didn't want Mercury around they would actually punish people for using it.

Through a loop and down a slide as I wiggle the Mercury around the glass. It needs to get all around the glass to make the Argon gas function better. A small speck of Mercury left behind on each part of the curved tube as it makes its way towards the end. After it coats everything I melt away the edge of the tubulated electrode that once held the corrupting element. Even though the bubble of Mercury is gone, it will stay with the tube, long after the gas gets absorbed into walls of glass, the transformer going out, electrical wire failure. It can't be used again for anything else as it has been poisoned unlike the pure Neon lights which can be used again and again. But it gave a view better than any Neon ever gave.

The edge of my blowhose hits the end of my phone in my shirt pocket as it starts to vibrate. A new message from Aaron, he probably is going to start practice now.

Aaron: Remember that kid Zack that was trying for first. Said he is probably gonna quit.

John: Y

Aaron: Not gonna be able to play. Can't take my spot even though he fields better I hit way better. I'm more valuable there coach said. Can't play infield cause he's lefthanded. Doesn't know how to play outfield. If he can't get playing time then wasting his time he says. He's a senior said he would do something else than waste time sitting on bench.

I put the Neon sign down back on the work desk. I'm ending a baseball career. Almost certainly at least a decade of baseball coming to an end because of me. A sudden ending that wasn't even thought to be an ending last year. No chance of becoming a professional anymore. Years of two hours a day of practice in the spring and for some people more, hours all year around just stopping now. Since he transferred he probably hoped he'd make the team but the moment I started sign stealing that ended baseball for him. I ended baseball for him. No chance of ever being on the field again. The phone screen goes dark from lack of response.

I hold in my hands the ability to end careers and pathways through life. You want to be a pitcher? I'm standing right in your way and you are not good enough to get around me. Got a hundred mile an hour fastball? Beat that two days ago. Lofty curveball done that. You have pin point pitch accuracy? Then you have no chance against me. I can make even the worst hitter imaginable into a superstar. And you don't have a single clue of the power I have.

Aaron: Our first away game's tomorrow.

Should I stop? I can't stop, if I stop now it's over. I would be benching Aaron and that would be it. Aaron's done so well on the last two games. A new bat, batting over five hundred, a homerun, and he is moving up the lineup. I can't let him throw away what he has and what he can do.

What about the careers of people who want to continue? What happens to those kids whose careers and futures I end?

I jiggle the Mercury to the end of the tube. Connect the electrodes to a sample transformer, customer will use their own power source. A gorgeous blue around the tube.

Baseball and really sports in general are the one escape for so many people. Financial escape from poverty. Not many opportunities to break free from hardship where you are? Sports are an equalizer among the rich and poor if you are willing to sacrifice your body for the entertainment of millions. Just have the body and ability to play and sports give you freedom. Sports give you emotional escape. Life at home bad? Come on down to the ballpark and forget all about that for the time you're there. Get excited over people hitting a baseball and running around bases. Get engrossed with the stats of the players. Will this be a homerun next pitch? Be a part of the action and forget about your mundane boring life. Some people out there think sports are really just people running around, but it is so so so much more than that.

I might have to end someone's career by what I do. Close out escapes and give them to Aaron. There are only a limited number of tickets to escape that any sport can give out to people. I've already closed out one for one person. I am going to have to close out a whole lot more. So much money from playing, so much that I wouldn't have to worry like my parents did so many times. What if no one comes into the store, what if I lose work at the police station. I even remember staring at my baseball ceiling worrying those things, what if no one goes into my dad's store, what if my mom loses her job. A whole lot of exit tickets are going to have to be taken away. I won't let Aaron or me ever have to worry like that again.

John: I'll be there.

I've played in every park that is on the schedule almost all of them have a chain link fence I can put the telescope right behind, but a few of them like the next one have some problems. Matted padding in the outfield, multiple bushes along the outfield fenceline, one even has a building acting as the center field wall.

The next Neon sign to make uses multiple letters all connected together, have to plan the exact markers on where to heat the glass so I can make the glass do what I need it to do. Start to mark up powdered yellow glass as I decide where I need to put the curves to make the sign show the lettering the way it needs to be seen. Brush aside the bushes maybe? Get on top of the roof of the building? Continue to mark up the glass. Planning is crucial for signing to work. Maybe for the padded outfield I can go with bringing a small elevation system and an extender tripod. Perhaps I could see if there is a nearby structure that I can place this on top of that gives me a better view?

I finished the markings and start applying heat to the glass. It doesn't have a clue it is about to bend.

Chapter 11

My dad's car beeps as I back it into the visitor's parking of West Charisma City High School. The main student parking is locked until school ends in a few minutes and the visitor parking isn't too much of a walk to the baseball field. Set into park as I look towards the back to see my laptop, foldable boxes, telescope and a different tripod to mount the telescope. First time out of my home turf, higher chance of not working, but I've practiced this last night.

The math will work because it is math. The glass and settings on the telescope will always show the same thing at a set distance, need a different distance, change a lens or adjust a focus knob. Three hundred seventy feet to center field from the online satellite set the telescope five feet behind the fence at a height of ten feet minus one foot catcher sign height creates a length of distance of view just a little over three hundred eighty when you count a catcher being behind the plate almost four feet. Almost looking straight ahead at around an eighty-eight degree angle to the catcher. Fence height of eight feet ensures that it won't block the view.

Presetted adjustments to the telescope to see at that range. Fully charged laptop, three foldable boxes one for the laptop and two for the telescope and tripod with multiple height settings, emergency computer extension cord in case it can't reach, but it will reach, I practiced the motion twice. Go set up boxes, make sure they are secure and will not collapse or blow away with a high wind. Step on one to get to the top of the stacked one, place the tripod with preset attachments and firmly ground it to the box. Connect computer and ensure that telescope is aimed properly at the imaginary catcher. You won't be able to see the catcher there but you know where exactly he is going to be and his distance. It will look blurry at first but don't panic when the catcher arrives he will be in full focus of me and that ICU bat.

I grab the items and place them coordinated in my right arm. Pinch on my elbow as it holds all the weight. My left hand is too weak for all of this, just have to push through the few thousand feet to the outfield fence. Even though it's a short walk through campus to the field, I have to walk around the entire ballpark just to get to center field. After the game's over I have to take it down and carry it right back the same way I came.

Lock the car door, and walk towards the entrance. The asphalt still cool during the bright day as January slowly yields to February. Sun overhead and won't mess with the telescope. For future games where the sun is behind home plate and hitting the lens will either place a covering over the telescope to shade from direct sunlight or other anti-glare reduction measures. Orange vested supervisor at the gate to the school. Stay calm might wonder what I am doing with this.

"Hang on," he says putting his hand out stopping me. Does he suspect what I am doing? I'm operating the camera on campus, could they know? "Have to wait for the bell."

No suspicion. I blow air past my lips. No longer a student just a visitor. An intruder that is entering a world that he is no longer allowed in, that he can't enter if he wanted to. Not a student they are worried about ditching class or going missing. No longer worried about my test scores, my plans, my attendance. No longer their problem. Just an element of the outside that could be contaminating things as he goes along.

Ding Ping Ding. The supervisor lets me through just as students start leaving portable classrooms, buildings and the gym. Walk through the crowd leaving, students mingling, some people going to another room even though school is out, maybe talking to a teacher, going to an after school club or getting ready for a sport.

Pass a few kids with baseball bats as they walk towards the locker room. They always wait until school gets out to start pregame practice. Away team gets to get out early to get to the field on time. Sometimes it's only a few minutes, other times you can get an hour or more on a bus ride and miss the last class period.

Walk past a few students relaxing on grass as the school slowly gets more open towards the athletic fields. Will any of these kids know what is going on? Are they going to tell anyone? Who would they tell? Could they put the process together if they see the laptop and the telescope? Just keep going, they aren't going to do anything. People who know baseball will be watching the games from the seats behind home plate. They aren't going to be relaxing out on the grass between the baseball and the tennis court.

Pinch on my arm again, hand off two boxes to my left hand. First member of the home team showing up towards the front of the field. West Charisma City on the jersey. Purple and green colored cap, ready to go.

Better hurry before more show up. I pass the edge of the right field fence and make the turn just as a few long distance runners pass me on their run around the campus. Track is in the same season as baseball. They don't know baseball so they don't know what's going on. Five seconds in front of the laptop screen during a run, they won't know what's going on. A limited audience with limited security with a performance that's life changing. And no one knows it's getting stolen.

Right behind centerfield, here we go. Unfolded box, Unfolded box, Unfolded box. Stacked up. Steady, tripod set up. Laptop turn on. Password input. Connected. Lens cap removed, Blurry backstop but that's ok. Math is working. Phone connected. Image on phone good. Connection will last the distance walking around back to the bleachers behind home. Centerfield padding defeated.

Last step to make sure no one touches it. Pull out back pocket and unfold paper that says do not touch. Dangerous while in use. Attach to second box. More players arriving, got to get there before mom and dad show up. If they get there before I do, just say I went to look for a restroom.

Simply having a piece of paper that says do not touch is begging them to actually touch it, especially if the thing not to touch looks simple. There are some people around here and someone is bound to be curious. However, if you tell people that something is dangerous while in use they will think it's ok to touch it when it's off, and that's why they can't touch it. If they see the laptop on they will see it's in use and leave it alone.

Walk towards the edge of the right side of the field as I see a few of the opposing team take warmups. Catcher with his leg guards taking his warmups with the pitcher. Every single time you are the starting pitcher you take your warmups with your catcher for the day. Get to work together to see what's working and what's not. Flips glove towards the catcher. Fastball. Glides his glove in his left hand across his body. Slider. Asks for money with his glove. Curveball. More kids coming out as I start to pass their dugout. He might have more but probably not, just be aware during the first at-bats of the team to see if he has anything.

My voice hurt after the last game when I sat at the top. Sit near the front so Aaron can hear me without me having to yell. Two rows up and I can place my legs against the back of the next seat. My parents are bound to be arriving soon just have to make sure to save them a seat in case more people start to show up.

It starts to warm up just as pregame warm-ups start to finish. As my parents walk up Aaron called them over to the dugout to tell them he was batting fifth. I was thinking he would be batting fourth already but it has been only two games of hitting. Need to make sure that it's not just a hot streak. Don't worry coach, Aaron is going to be on fire for the entire year.

Opposing pitcher takes the mound. Looks average size five seven, fastball maybe upper sixties lower seventies. He won't make it after this year. Looks like a senior. Standard overhand delivery with slightly scrawny shoulders that puberty didn't expand. That means less potential fastball speed from biometric physical limitations.

Randy, first batter up watch the pitches. Make sure that he doesn't have anything that surprises. One two three fingers down. Does he not have a change-up or is he using his curveball as a change-up? Line drive between the third base hole. Sean up second, still no change-up, grounder to second, gets out at second. Third batter up big hit over the first baseman's head. Cheering from the crowd rounds first and slides into second with plenty of time.

That could make things tougher to move past fifth in the lineup. Runner third and second. If the guy playing third base can get a solid hit here he is gonna be staying in fourth for a while. Ball one. There is a change-up. Just a tad slower but not much and you can kinda tell from how he pitches it's just a tad different on a change-up. Curveball strike. I glance back at the telescope in center. I can't see if anyone behind the padding is looking at it. Just have to wait and see if anything happens. Ball two.

Oh man, he is more likely to hit this ball now. As the count gets towards a hitter because there are more balls, he has a better chance of getting a base hit. He can choose the pitch to hit, pitcher doesn't want to give a walk. Ball three. Take the next pitch. Walk give Aaron his first chance with the bases loaded. Catcher sets up outside will be willing to give up walk don't want to give up a hit and let runs score. Perfect spot and a ball.

Double play depth the catcher shouts. Oh please, you really think that is gonna happen with Aaron at the plate. More likely to get struck by lightning than to turn two right now. Corners in. Aaron at the plate. Let's get a Grand Slam now. First one of the year and many more to come.

The ICU bat gleams it eyes at me, the pitcher, and the telescope behind the wall in center. Its blue shade tints with the daylight.

"Get a base hit Arron!" my mom shouts. "Give it your best hack out there Aaron," I signal to him. Just a bit inside with the fastball. "Let's go Aaron," the change-up tucks just on the outside part of the plate. He takes a step outside the box and rolls his shoulders. Right back in.

Two fingers down and a brush towards Aaron, "wait for your pitch if you have to Aaron." From the windup, the pitcher moves his foot forward and up, lurches forward with an L arm and lets go. Aaron locked on the pitch and punches it way over the first baseman's head.

Not enough power to get out of here. My head goes into my left hand. Bounce bounce then thuds against the padding. Runners running. Sean rounds third easy. Aaron rounding first just as the right fielder gets the ball. First base runner midway past second waved towards home plate. First base has the cutoff. Past third ball coming in bounce and he slides wide of the plate and tag. Lurches towards the plate and gets it with the edge of his batting glove. Safe. Only three runs scored.

I snap my fingers down. That was a good pitch to hit too and only a double. My head swings back without a headrest to stop it.

"How can you be mad at that?" my dad asks. "He got a double and scored three runs. Want him to strikeout?" he tilts his body towards me demanding an answer.

I point the obvious, "it just could have been a grand slam."

"You know how hard it is to hit a homer?"

I remark, "he got one last time, they should be easy for Aaron. Guy like this, we need to be getting homeruns like crazy against guys like him."

My mom shakes her head at me as the next batter takes the plate. Eric batting sixth groundout and seventh a flyout to strand Aaron at second, inning over.

Batters up, and down runs score and runners held on. Third inning no one on two outs. Aaron up one more time. Let's get a homerun this time. Shaky pitcher probably going to get pulled after this inning, let's actually send one over the fence with this guy before he gets pulled.

Sun has moved slightly but still not blocking the camera view. Fastball low and away. Ball one good take. Change-up inside. Free swinging now kid. Free swinging now kid. Catcher sets up on the inner part of the plate but sure for a strike. The pitcher goes through his wind-up trying for a change of pace. Strike one. One-one. Gotta take some swings. Catcher signals one yes wiggles right no wiggles left no. Puzzled catcher flicks his right hand towards the pitcher. Yes fastball up sets up outside in a half standing position. "Gotta take command out there."

Pitch comes and the ICU makes strong contact. Straight to center. Gliding losing steam center fielder gives chase. Almost out and it's out just over the wall. Homerun. Aaron turns his run into a trot just as he rounds first base. One more RBI to add to the record. The opposing team signals to one of the guys on the bench to go get the ball from the outfield. There's someone going behind the fence. There's someone going behind the fence! I jolt from my seat and start running down the bleachers.

"I need to get Aaron's homerun ball. We have to keep that for the memory." Oh man he has a head start ahead of me. At least thirty seconds. Clug Clug down the end of the steps as I get off the bleachers. I haven't run in so long. Pass the home dugout as fast as I can. He can't make it to behind centerfield. He'll see the camera! The benchwarmer swings around the side of the bullpen just as the pitcher there finishes up getting ready for relief. Worry about him later.

Ping from a bat just as he gets beyond the pen towards right field. "UP UP UP!" I shout. Instinctively the benchwarmer goes down and takes cover not knowing where the ball is. The catcher and the pitcher look weirdly at both of us. Keep going. Cramp in side of my stomach. Don't care keep running pass him up just as he starts to look around for the ball.

Ahead of him just get the ball before he sees the camera. Turn the corner behind the fence and cramp in my stomach gets worse. I haven't ran since baseball ended. Need to exercise. Gentle curve around the edge of the fence just blocking the view a few dozen feet ahead. Where is the ball? That kid must have started running and probably is getting laughed at by his teammates for ducking for no reason. The ball probably was just a grounder.

The ball stopped a few feet beside the camera, thank goodness. Pick up the ball, slightly worn from being hit. In high school they don't change the ball each time it gets hit like they do in the professional leagues. It would be way to expensive to do that in a high school level. Though they occasionally will get a few dozen balls every so often.

Start jogging back just as the benchwarmer gets closer to me. Stop him right there go closer so he stops. Five six shortest guy on their team but still taller than me. Black hair looks like a junior based on his small physicality, hope he gets some playing time soon and just doesn't have to be fetching foul balls all day.

"Why did you say that ball was popped up?" Oh no, he's suspicious.

Shooting out a response, "because I wanted this one." I wave the ball around as I start to walk back towards the bleachers. Just get him away from the camera, he would realize what was going on.

He steps towards me, "we need that ball back. Wait you're Aaron Base's brother aren't you?" I nod yes. Is he getting more suspicious? Keep him away from the camera. "Heard what he did against Anthony from West Chestlake high. Looks like Aaron's unstoppable right now." You don't know anything. But you can't start questioning.

"Our coach still needs that ball back. You know we don't have that many baseballs to go around, we can't just let any ball that leaves the yard go to the guy that hits it."

I need to put up a fight to get him to think it wasn't weird what I did. "No way this is Aaron's. It's a homerun ball."

He drops his shoulders, "oh wow, that's why you embarrassed me a second ago. Aaron wants that ball so bad he tells his brother to go run and scare off anyone who is getting the ball."

I hold the ball close to my chest, "you'd tell someone to get the ball if you ever hit a homerun. Want it so bad? Take it, I don't care I am getting the next one though."

Blows air out of his mouth, "the next one? He just got lucky right there." I toss him the ball as he turns around, "let me tell you what, if he gets another he can keep it."

Exhale and take a knee to catch my breath from the excitement of what happened. I realize that this is going to be a lot tougher than it seemed to be. Each time now there is a homerun and not just Aaron's, I'll have to race and stop some person from seeing the camera. I have to find a way to disassemble the system at the end of the game without anyone noticing, the other team, my parents, random bystanders.

At the end of each away game from now on, I have to run off from my parents in the bleachers, make an excuse, disassemble the system, put it in the car and run back before anyone sees. Getting caught is the worst case scenario. I heave once more as I get up to go back to the bleachers. Just tell Aaron if an at-bat is at the end of an away game, I can't help him. It will only be one at-bat every so often, but it will be impactful. Seventh inning you're up, I can't help you. But maybe it won't be so bad if you get three homeruns earlier in the game.

Chapter 12

Aaron's email box is filled with subscriptions to science websites and school assignments but the one he wanted to show me is coming from a university email address.

Dear Aaron Base,

This is coach Jeremiah from Sorbluff State University. I currently am the hitting coach here at Sorbluff State and I have received news of your amazing hitting ability so far this year. As of this email I read that you have hit eleven homeruns in only seven games and are currently batting just over .821. I want to see you in action and I'm planning on going to one of your games week after next. Want to talk about the Sorbluff State Baseball program after? I don't want to change a single thing on how you swing. It seems perfect the way it is.

Coach J

We got a bite. It's not a professional team but it is something. At the pace we are going we are going to get a lot more people wanting to watch us play. Team managers, Athletic Directors, maybe even an owner of a team.

I lean over the end of Aaron's desk, "wow it looks like Coach J is going to try and recruit you over to Sorbluff University."

"Go Sorbluff U," Aaron chuckles as he opens a webpage to their website.

A picture of their chemistry lab shows up on screen, "you know they don't pay you in college baseball right?" Picture of their quad, then their dormitories and a library.

Aaron sighs as he closes the window, "I know but still, college is expensive and a scholarship might do a bit to get me over there."

"Yeah, but what happens when I can't help anymore and you lose your scholarship after a year? They are not letting you go there for free, they expect you to play just as well as you are now. It was crazy enough to set up the telescope at the last two away games. Once I'm not there you miss every pitch. Even if I wanted to pay for your college this way, how could I pay for me going over there living near Sorbluff State? How could I even leave something like that, a telescope, in center at a real stadium?"

He closes the laptop and sighs, "think anyone else is gonna send some messages?"

I respond to calm him down, "of course they're going to, it's only been a little more than a fifth of the season done so far, seven games done and we got someone this quick."

His head goes into his hand as he falls back into his chair, "how much longer do I have to do this?"

"Twenty-eight games left in the season. We're done on graduation week." That's the last time I'm out on the field. The last time I will be watching everything.

I hear the mail slot click open and swing back closed. Mail here. I leave Aaron at his desk as I go to see if there is any mail for me. Ever since my dad had me working in the shop, he's been giving me more of an understanding of the rules of the business. Even though customers see one thing, there actually is a whole lot of stuff going on behind the scenes to make sure everything is working. Business regulations, tax laws, customer invoices, all important and all full of paperwork. Sometimes we get paperwork for the business at our house, though usually it is at the store.

I hear the flipping of papers by the kitchen table from my mom. Police regulations she has to read through, changes on zoning regulations, city council notifications. Paperwork paperwork paperwork. I grab the half dozen pieces of mail off the carpet and start to dice through the mail.

Tax forms, acknowledgement of buzzer purchases, marketing material. Letter for Aaron with the logo of the Steel Springs Moon Craters! They want to know something about him. The Moon Craters, a professional baseball team, are sending us personal letters. These are the people that we need to be hearing from.

"Aaron come over here!" I shout.

My mom puts her papers down and takes a look at me. Aaron's door creaks open as he takes a step out.

I wave the unopened letter for Aaron in the air to show him. We have a professional organization who noticed. Not some college who isn't gonna pay because it's too stingy to pay its athletes. Straight onto becoming a pro, getting a large signing bonus. Don't dedicate yourself to any team, just go for the one that has the most money. If your planning on being a long term athlete, unless you're going to be the greatest of all time and actually want to be that kind of player, go for the team that will make you the most money as soon as you can. You don't know how long your career can last.

One injury can destroy your career. One mistake can cost you a contract. Every single play evaluated to determine your career. One bad day can bench you for the rest of your career and then, that's it. It's all over. The player on the bench takes your spot after going on a hot streak. He or she takes your spot on the field, then you're let go because you don't have a chance to go back in, even if you are just as good you used to be. The money stops and you're just like everyone else watching the game on the television.

Your ability to play a sport doesn't count for much on a resume outside sports, maybe manual labor. But the money you made while playing if you went with the team that paid you the most, could last multiple lifetimes for yourself, your family and your kids for potentially generations. All because you had the physique and could hit a baseball, tackle someone, kick a soccer ball better than most other people. You probably won't be remembered by people or fans after you leave the sport, but your money will be remembered by those you care about long after you step off the field.

Aaron grabs the letter from me and takes a look at the front, "Steel Springs is almost a two day drive away from here." He tears open the letter, peeling the edge of the seal off tarnishing the logo.

"Well? What's it say about my swinging slugger?" my mom asks as she hugs him.

Aaron looks at me, "what do you think it says John?"

I bite my teeth down, what would they actually say. It's obvious they are interested. Word has to be getting around now because he is on pace to smash nearly every record that he can actually participate in.

Crossing my fingers, "they are reserving you a first round draft pick?"

"Almost, they want to see if I keep it up for two or three more games, they are gonna send a scout to watch."

If they are sending someone this early they are definitely thinking of spending their first round pick on him. They are mid round picks with at least some money to spend. Their first baseman is retiring this year or next, so they are probably looking for a replacement to take over for a while.

My mom hugs Aaron harder, her face smushing against his upper bicep, "oh wow a scout. They are finally seeing the potential of my special man." They don't have a clue what is going on behind the scenes of this.

Chapter 13

Fastball outside. Ball one. Sean on first base taking a slight lead against the righty. One out to start the game. This is a perfect time to get another RBI. At the pace we're going we are probably gonna double the league record of RBIs from forty to eighty. Each homerun Aaron gets is one ribbie but with a runner on he doubles it. Even if it isn't a homerun, ball in the outfield still has a chance of bringing someone in.

Change-up outside down, "let's go Aaron." Pitcher begins his motion from the stretch and Sean takes off. Aaron takes, catcher pops up and fires Sean slides into second just ahead of the tag. A few milliseconds difference and he would have been out.

That's strange, Sean never had the green light from coach last season, only Randy and I did. Stealing a base is pretty risky, you risk an out to get either into scoring position or get to third base. Granted that boosts your chances of scoring but outs are valuable. There is a big difference between two outs in an inning and one out. But even if you get the stolen base you still have to have someone hit you in. Made Aaron's job just a little easier.

One-one change-up inside. "Free swinging now kid." Sean taking a huge lead off second base. Shortstop holding him on. Pitcher looks once and twice. Leg up and pitch released Sean bolts to third base. Ball hits catcher's glove quick grab fires to third, safe just under the tag.

It's actually easier to steal off a change-up than a fastball because of the time it actually takes to reach home plate. If a ball is going around eighty miles an hour it takes a little more than half a second to get home once the pitcher releases the ball. If the ball is going only seventy miles an hour because of a change-up to make the batter miss on his timing, then it takes almost a sixtieth of a second to get there. If you run reasonably fast at four and a half steps a second that means you get a half a step advantage over the catcher. That's a huge difference stealing a base. Did you have a good jump off first? No, well if you are running against a change-up you might still just have a chance.

Coach is shaking his head at Sean as he takes his lead off of third base. Definitely no green light, but how is he stealing a base? He was never that kind of bold on the basepaths, always just listening to the coaches telling him to go, hold up, and sometimes not even going on a steal sign.

Always worried about risks and chance. Stealing third is even riskier. The distance to the base is shorter and a catcher has to throw only ninety feet to third but almost a hundred and thirty to second. Smaller distance same arm speed you have to take every advantage you can get to steal third without just wasting an out. Get out on the basepaths, you just lost a runner. Out at third, lost a runner in scoring position.

Is he going to steal home? Ok Aaron if he is stealing home don't swing. I don't care, I have to see this. Kid running home batter swinging that ends in catastrophe. Line drive towards a guy running twelve miles an hour towards the ball coming at him at a hundred. Don't run or don't swing one of you. Curveball outside low. "Show him what that ICU bat can do now kid." Don't steal home now. Do not try and steal every base.

From the windup not caring about the runner anymore. The hurler steps towards home leg outstretches and his wrist snaps the ball towards the plate. Ball starts to tumble but the ICU bat saw the pitch from a mile away. Bang! Going way back into the center left gap, outfielders give up chase. Going gone. Ball bounces on the concrete street and hits a parked car about ten doors down from my house. That's fifty bucks on the school's insurance policy to fix that dent. Better get up to walk the ball in. Sean waves off a high five from the fourth batter, I think Aaron told me his name is Nathan.

Since Aaron has been hitting so many homeruns I've convinced the coach to let me walk and get any homeruns that happen on home games. Saves me and a bench warmer from racing to get the ball. Though the away games can be a workout for me. Ready to bolt at any moment.

Sean takes a look at Aaron's bat, Aaron's gonna be mad at him for touching it but he'll get over it. Rounds second and halfway through his trot. Sean stares at the outfield towards my house and then back at the eyes of the bat glaring right back at him. ICU. Rounds third and touches home. Nathan fist bumps Aaron and Sean leaves Aaron hanging as he shakes his head at him. Both walk back to the dugout Aaron with his ICU bat and Sean glaring back and forth at Aaron and the outfield. Two fingers up then three fingers then a jaw dropping snap.

Just as I get to the edge of the dugout all I see is Sean staring at me as the game keeps getting called.

Chapter 14

Five fifty. Practice ended a few minutes ago and I am about to close up shop for dad. Finishing making vector signals for the signs tomorrow. Create extra symbols for more bizarre signs in the case we have to deal with those. Wiggle and jiggles where we don't even know what the outcome is going to be.

The door dings, "Zackery quit because of me," chang ching, "I don't want to see any more people's dreams shattered because of this." Zackery quit baseball. My sign stealing scandal created the first official known casualty. Zack quit because he didn't get any playing time with Aaron. There may be other people who quit because of this. Pitcher who is bench warming because he gave up hits to Aaron and lost a game. Pitcher got moved around the bullpen because of Aaron or is no longer pitching at all.

"What's he gonna do now then?" I ask.

"I don't know he turned in his jersey back to the coach and said that was it. That guy loved baseball, this is the last stop for most kids and I took it away." Don't take it away from me either Aaron. I've gotten to focus and watch every game so far this season. Each homerun and double, solid contact has been amazing this year.

Zack probably is going to look for something else to do for the last few months of his senior year. Maybe he might decide to do something else on the campus. Maybe he might forgo that all together and just finish the classes and graduate in a few months. Just go home and do homework watch television. Baseball probably won't be on the screens at his house anymore.

I bite my lip, "what are you going to do?" Is Aaron going to quit to? Please no. Please no. Please no. This is the ticket to millions of dollars, just put up with this for a few months Aaron. You don't realize how much is on the line for you to keep doing this. Your parents not having to worry about their future. You not having to worry about money.

"Stick out the season but just don't cheat anymore. There isn't anyone whose big enough to play first on the team coach said." That's even worse than quitting. We were doing so well and you're throwing it away. For what? You have already been cheating since the start of the season. There is so much money that they are getting ready to bring to the table.

"A scout was coming to your next home game." Maybe that could convince him to keep going. A potential baseball future. I would have begged for a chance at that.

He shakes his head at me and points to put the telescope back on the shelf. He doesn't want it. He goes towards the back of the shop to see if there are any tasks that dad wrote for him to do before he goes home and starts homework.

No arguing with Aaron. He starts moving the two hundred pound sheets of metal that I couldn't lift today. The sheets of metal screech in pain as they get dragged for a moment on the floor then lifted with ease. Why does Aaron have that kind of strength and not use it? So much potential just from his size that I don't even have. Just a few more inches on my height could have solved a lot of my problems in baseball. Problems in life even.

People love people who are taller. They're treated nicer. They are the good guys in movies. They get respect from people simply by being tall and doing nothing else. They have abilities in most sports over shorter people that shorter people can't do anything about. If you're short you have disadvantages that you can't make up. Stuck having to work twice as hard and still not be given chances. Maybe the reason the short people are the bad guys in the movies, is because they don't have the opportunity to be the good guys.

Aaron moves the next sheets over as he starts putting panes of glass on racks by the shelf. Moving the gas equipment towards its storage spots. Using that ability just to move simple items around.

I can't convince Aaron to continue to do this now but I need to soon. You shouldn't be wasting ability like that. I can't be wasting that potential like that just being used for lifting pieces of glass around. I'll have to watch Aaron take his strikeouts until there's a way to convince him to actually let me steal signs again.

Chapter 15

Dirt and dust brush into the bin when the front door dings open just as the clock ticks to four. Customer again, broom goes back in its place away from the paint supplies. Customers' orders going in and out like clockwork, smooth production for this month until we hit a snag earlier. Go into the front and I see my catcher Sean standing near the door.

"Shouldn't you be at practice?" I ask. Sean's brown hair is still oily even without the effects of his catcher mask.

He looks around the store and sees no one else here, "I should be, but something's more important. Is your dad here right now?"

"Just me," he turns around and flips the open sign to closed.

"We are still open for customers," I take a stand in front of the counter.

"I don't think you want anyone hearing what I am about to say." Is this a secret order, secret message? I think Sean's mom might own a music store here in town. Does she want a secret sign design no one else can know about?

He starts to move closer to the counter but he is apprehensive, not sure how to say what he is about to say, "you know, I played catcher since tee-ball. Always when everyone is facing the batter, I am facing the pitcher and the entire field. I can see the infielders and move them around, occasionally I would tell the outfield to move around a bit. Move up move back. But every single pitch I'm looking out not looking in like everyone else is. I'm not looking at the batter and pitcher. I'm just looking at the pitcher and the field outside. Every pitch always the same, sure different pitchers around, maybe a side-armer here or someone with a weird pitch. But it is always the same. Then this year I noticed something different. Something that no one looks at. Past the fence of the outfield."

What's he getting at? Be vague. "Um, you noticed the seasons changing?" Does he know about the sign stealing?

"You have a really nice house John," he says.

"You noticed my house?" Ok that's good, just stay on this pathway. Weird, but just stay on this way. This way makes no sense, but it's away from what I am doing.

"Not your house but where it is. It's right out in center field, you have the perfect view of every game, better than a television spot. In your front yard I noticed a telescope, something kinda like the ones you have on the shelf. And a computer." He knows.

Be as calm as I can force myself, "there was a computer and a telescope in front of my house." Know exactly what he knows.

"Not just at your house, but every single away game as well so far this year. There is a telescoped aimed right at me every game. It sees me. But why would anyone have open eyes for some dude giving out pitching signs everyday? I sat around the dugout and thought, maybe they aren't looking at me each time but the other guy on the other team. At first it didn't make sense. Then I realized how well Aaron Base was doing. Aaron Base the kid who shouldn't have made varsity, suddenly on track to double the homerun record. Aaron Base the best batter in the league from a total zero. Aaron Base who lives across the street from the field."

"You should let Aaron hear that."

"I don't think I will, look how big that guy is. But I am telling you because I think those two things go together. And it is because of you. I realized something John. Even though kids in the dugout were shouting. I also heard you. And somethings just didn't make sense. You've told Aaron to wait for his pitch on a two strike count at least four times. You're a pitcher, You played baseball for years and you know that makes no sense. Unless that's not what you're really saying. There is a code you're doing. Over the last few games I noticed depending on the pitch and even where it was gonna get thrown you shout out the same exact thing."

Caught. Don't say anything. If you don't say anything nothing will happen.

"I didn't want to believe it when I first thought it, but I wanted to test it. I bat right before Aaron and when I got on base I heard you and knew what pitch was coming too. Or at least I thought I did. If I was right, I could know. So I risked it; if it wasn't a breaking pitch I was wrong, and you just are glued to your phone while you miss your brother have the greatest senior year ever. But if I was right and I stole a base, then I just uncovered the biggest fraud in my life. I got into second on the nick of time and it was a change-up. Was I right? Needed to make sure. So, I took third base and I was right. Aaron knew every single pitch. That's how Aaron Base, the worst baseball player in the world became a superstar. I'd be just like him if I knew what the pitchers were throwing."

Lighten the mood. "Very interesting theory you're saying." He just stares at me. Is he going to demand I help him too? Help the whole team cheat? That's too many people.

"John stop lying to me for once. You lied about your arm pain and now you're lying about this." He just wants to be serious.

"Did Aaron tell you?"

"Aaron's behind this? I knew it. I figured he was the one behind the scheme. He is the one playing after all." Checks to see my reaction, nervous looking around. "Look it just needs to stop. It needs to stop, you need to tell your brother to stop cheating."

"This can't stop Sean," the season can't end like this, we are doing amazing. Day in day out amazing outcomes, scouts are talking about us. End now and that stops immediately.

"You're destroying dreams out there John. Every single pitcher out there is getting served on a platter for Aaron by you. Without you, Aaron is nothing. The kids on the team, if I told them they wouldn't believe me, they probably would think I'm crazy. I doubt that coach will do anything."

No one will believe him. No one wants to believe him. No one wants to think the people at the top are a bunch of cheats and crooks even though they really are. The ones playing like Sean aren't gonna be the professionals. The superstars. People won't even believe him if he tells the truth.

"I need to reopen the store, it was good pitching for you all those years," I say as I walk to open the door. I need a moment to cool off, this is too crazy.

Sean starts to follow me out the store, his attempt failed not sure what to do now. The greatest scheme of all time and no one will believe him if he said what happened. Everyone duped for a brief moment in time and the only people not duped were the people that weren't watching the game.

Chapter 16

Crowding the plate with the thirty-two inch bat because I am too small to reach the other side of the plate, too weak to control a thirty-three inch bat, I get ready for the next screwball from the avatar righty. Leg up and the pitch comes towards me, the ball starts to turn just slightly towards me as I make core contact with the middle of the bat. Sharp hit towards the hole between shortstop and third base, or at least where they would be if this was a game.

Aaron wants to stop, Sean knows about what is going on and wants to tattle, dad wants his telescope back. All the things on the plate and there is nothing I can do now but wait for the pitch and see if anything happens.

I push through the elbow sting as I take another swing at the baseballs. Making contact, machine says most are not making it out of the infield even with an upwards launch. Another swing as every other batting cage is being taken over by a youth team taking turns before a game somewhere else.

Even though it can be costly, going to the batting cages as a team could be an effective hitting practice. Typically you can rent a cage for an hour, if you rent multiple cages you can have multiple hitters hitting. In most standard practices, you can only have one or maybe two people hitting for safety reasons, but with a batting cage you can have as many people hitting as you have cages. Granted you typically want them to take a break every so often so you don't need a cage per person. Maybe one for every four kids.

Maybe I remind Aaron of the money, maybe I tell Aaron about how much stress our parents are under? Maybe I tell him of the fame he could get? Maybe I tell him that somewhere out there, there is a guy who is just as good as him doing the exact same thing to other players without cheating and would he care about that?

Take another turn in the batting cage. Elbow stings but hitting can be relaxing. Ball going in and right off the sweet spot of the bat doesn't cause too much sting. Neck tilts each time the ball comes in. First towards the pitcher, then towards the bat, then the back towards where the ball went.

More kids cycling through the batting changes. First two pitches bunts then swinging away. I used to be able to put the ball anywhere on the infield. A little out of practice as I take a swing and send the ball towards the shortstop hole. Maybe a single. But even if I could constantly get singles I am still stuck at first base always. Someone has to do something to bring me in. I can't do this myself. Fastball low and away.

Swing and a crackle from the bat as the clock says that it is almost six o'clock. They probably are going to be closing in thirty minutes. I've been here almost all day taking swings with this bat on my day off. Dad holding down the shop on days that are expected to be very slow. Got a discount from the manager and technician when I first showed up and they let me take over an entire batting cage for hours.

Another slap at the ball and a crack appears near the handle of the bat. I swung so many times I almost broke a bat. The wrapped handle starts to leech out small particles of composite. Ball hits the tarp. I put so much work into this bat that it is no longer usable. Maybe another bat? But will they let me use another one after I pushed so hard on this one?

I exit the cage, marking my spot so the youth team can't take my cage. I got all day to use the cage for what I paid, I don't want to wait in line especially since I have to go home soon.

Walk up one more time to the counter. Jason Niagara on the television one more time about his season progress.

Slide the bat across the counter and point towards the damage, "need a new bat for the day."

The same worker from last time bulges his eyes open. "You broke the bat?!"

Please don't make me pay for it. I don't have money to pay to replace this. I might not even have any money for baseball after this. If Aaron doesn't want to keep taking signs then he won't be able to hit at all.

He takes a look at the bat itself, the handle just crippling itself each motion it takes, "wow someone like you broke it? Never would have guessed, but maybe it's from the amount of repetitive use in such a short time." Some lower quality bats end up losing their structural integrity after a few hundred hits, but some bats actually lose their hitting ability, their ability to make strong contact over time, after swings as well. The worst part is that you can't actually physically see the weakening of the bat through your eyes. The evidence of the weakened bat comes from seeing decreased ball travel distance, decreased exit velocity, thus worse hitting outcomes. It's a reason why you should spend and purchase a good quality bat instead of a cheap one. They tend to last longer and might actually keep you off the bench because you might just get an edge that keeps you in the lineup.

I tilt my neck towards my shoulder, muscle tightening from the sheer amount of turning while hitting, "do you have another one that I can use?" I look towards the back wall with a variety of different colored bats. Aaron tried out most of these, but all he didn't like them. Always something wrong with it for his hitting.

He slides the bats around the rack behind him, "want something end loaded? More weight maybe to gain muscle while swinging the bat?" He points towards my small triceps and shoulders. When I tried working out, with my natural metabolism, I hardly gained any muscle. Even after weeks and months of trying I couldn't put on muscle weight like bigger kids.

I look around the booth at other bats, "how about something for someone my size?" You actually use your hips to generate most of the power from hitting and pitching but arms do play some role. Either way though the more muscle mass you have the more potential you have for the ball to go far.

The five six worker strokes his chin as he inspects the bat, "hmmm, we have something new that might work. There is an unused two-piece bat in our newly received inventory." He pulls out his cell phone, "just give me a second, the manager left after lunch to meet with a bat company for getting a new shipment. Let me make a phone call to see if we can let you use it."

I look towards the kids taking turns in the cages as he begins to call on the phone. The smaller ones are using the two piece bat while the larger ones used the one pieces. Balls travel across the batting cages as balls are hit and missed.

I personally used the two piece bat when I played because since I was so short and crowded the plate, I would often hit the ball on the weaker part of the bat closer to the handle on inside pitches. With a two piece bat, you have more sting reduction as compared to a one piece. If I had to pitch right after I made contact near the handle my hands would be ringing just as I picked up the ball. It would be a lot harder to control the pitches, make the balls break more, and even get speed on the fastball which I really really needed.

The sound of the pitching machines roar over the area as the last batting cage gets taken over by an eleven year old who is wondering why I am hogging an empty batting cage. The technician smiles over the phone and gives a thumbs up to me and continues talking.

The disadvantage to the two piece bat is that it tends to have reduced outcomes than the one piece because it reduces potential sting on the hands. The reason the two piece bat works is because there is a connection between the first part of the bat handle and the barrel the second piece. The connection reduces sting but it also has a tendency to reduce baseball bat power.

Wrapping up the phone call as he puts the phone in his pocket, "he told me to go in the back and grab a prototype that one of our suppliers recently made. Two piece limited production for testing. The company says the bat is already prepped for hitting before they put the paint on. Look's like your the first person to actually test out this one." He turns his key on the cash register and rushes out of the stand and towards the back end of the store.

I guess that is the first good thing that has happened to me today. I get to take a few swings with a prototype baseball bat. Maybe my luck is breaking the slump. I'm not quite sure how true this is because I've never actually seen the baseball bat making process but I'd assume that these companies go through revisions before they go out for the general public for purchase. Take feedback from testers, see if the materials are acceptable, are they cost efficient for production.

I hear his footsteps just behind the noise of the store's sound system playing baseball songs. I always wished I had walk up music when I went up to bat. They always play it for professional players.

He walks back as he starts removing the plastic wrap of the ends of the white and blue bat. The front of the baseball bat says the word PAWN in big letters across the barrel, "it's a thirty-two inch bat that is meant for smaller people. I have a feeling this one in particular suits you." He starts to tear the last remaining pieces of tape of the end of the sleek bat handle. "My boss said that they are making a thirty-three inch one as well. He's been always having us review bat specifics like he wants us to make them.

Always says that he could make a better one, than any company. I don't believe him." He hands me the end of the bat to take a look.

Large barrel like most bats with the small black end cap followed by a quick two inch and a half solid bright blue all around. Then a clean white for the next two and a half inches marking the sweet spot of the bat. The end of the letter N made up of a diagonal pattern of blue and a brighter white right at in the middle of the sweet spot. The white of the N just slightly different from the rest of the slightly darker white. A corruption of the white that you can only notice if you look carefully.

The next letters in a similar solid chess board style color scheme until the end of the barrel piece of the bat. White and dark blue letters across a clear marking of light sky blue. A light white connection zone that looks like it can give significant cushion on a pitch merges the bat to the handle piece. A slim bright white area circling the entire bat before the handle has the bat information in blue typeface before the piece shrinks to the handle. Grip on the handle to prevent sting before ending with a white and blue striped knob. Look's real nice.

I grasp the snow white airated leathery grip of the bat, feels really nice, "oh believe me, he could definitely make the best bat possible." Right hand over left as I take a mock half swing away from the stand. Nicely balanced for hitting. "But this one just feels really good itself." The ICU bat had way more of an end load. I actually tried grabbing it before I came over here to take swings with it but Aaron was even more mad at me for grabbing it. Those eyes glared at me so I just decided to use the bats over here.

He points towards the striped end knob, "yeah the manager recently told me that the company is giving these out for limited public testing. The company wants feedback and how it goes to determine if they are sticking with the design for that model." He motions to see the bat one more time and I hand it back towards him.

Taking a grip of the handle, "I typically see your brother here. I wouldn't recommend a short bat for him because it lowers his hitting ability." He stares at me as I try and comprehend.

"It's because there are two types of goals when you are hitting. Making contact or hitting for power. We all should honestly try hitting for power but some of us," he points to my five four height and his five six height, “we just really can’t so instead we should just focus on making contact with the ball because we will be lucky to hit the ball into the middle of the outfield.”

Tosses the bat back towards me as he relocks the register and steps out of the booth. He waves his hand towards the batting cage that I was using. Wants to see how it hits. I step back into the cage and put my helmet back on.

Starts pushing buttons on the machine, “the bat you’re using is more even balanced than other one piece bats, it lets you have more bat control because of its balance,” the avatar of the pitcher begins to appear. Righty that is just a bit taller than me. “More bat control in this case means you can make contact a little easier, but you lose some power.” I get ready for the pitch as the wind-up comes in. Back shoulder drops front foot pivots and full frame of the bat crosses the plate as I hit the outside pitch.

Sharply hit towards the right side of the batting cage. Avatar gets another ball magically in his glove as he sets.

“Alright since my boss wants to try and see how well the bat works. I want to try something with you right now. I am going to select the pitches then I am going to tell you what pitch and where it’s gonna go. You got that.”

“Uh yeah, think so.” Oh man I get to know what it’s like to actually know what pitch is coming. Not behind the fence but actually at bat again. I imagine myself back in a game. One that I will never be in again but just as real as the other games. Randy on first base second baseman going to cover if he steals, have to advance the runner. “This one is going to be a fastball low and away about seventy miles an hour.” Let’s make some contact now John Base.

Pitch coming and I lean towards the outside part of the plate and slap it towards the hole. Runner advances and I am out at first. Ok do that one more time to move him over to third base.

“Next pitch same thing same spot.” The pitcher not knowing. I get to rev and make solid contact not having to lunge at the ball to make contact. Not unsettled with where the ball is going to be. Set and know what is going to happen. I love this.

Randy takes his lead and the avatar throws the same pitch again. Bang towards the right side of the field. Runner at third two outs drive this one back towards the pitcher. Get a base hit and you get a run. A homerun would be better but I can't get those, I'm just too small and weak.

"Curveball on the lower outside part of the plate." Ok focus on getting the sweet spot of the bat. Make good timing, and keep your weight balanced, end with weight just slightly on your front foot when the ball hits the bat.

Seams dip as I go through the main motion of my swing, forearms grip the handle tightly as the bat flows towards where the ball will be. Lined back just above the pitcher's head and a base hit towards center field. One run. "Fastball inside." Got to reset. Randy and Sean on first and third one out. Corners in double play depth mid fielders. Have to hit the ball between the short and third hole. Pitcher checks runners once. Slide step for a quick pitch. My front leg lands down a few inches towards third base and the barrel of the bat flows on the inside part of the plate. Ball hits the edge of the N on the bat and rockets between the third and shortstop hole.

Regrip the bat as I readjust for the next in game situation. Sean on third have to bunt him in. Safety squeeze. If it lands he runs in if not stay back.

"Change-up inside." Perfect pitch to bunt on. Hold back until last possible second don't let the third baseman charge early. Right hand glides just over onto the barrel piece of the bat. Ball coming. Right arm pushes forward and the ball ricochets along the line towards third base. He would have scored. Two runs. Free swinging John Base just make contact all around the field. Fastball up. Fastball outside. Up the middle ground ball. Curveball outside. Opposite field grounder down the line. Lefty curveball inside. Pulled down the line just fair. Pitches go by as the technician tells me more pitches and scribbles. Then suddenly to stop as they are about to close now. Avatar disappears one more time.

I'm sad. That's too bad. I was having fun. Getting to hit a baseball with a new bat. Getting base hits. He finishes writing notes about the bat in the booklet. Looks like I have to put this one back. I would have totally used this if I was still on the team.

The other kids have left and placed bats to return across the counter. I must have been too focused on hitting to notice. Not as much sting on my elbow as compared to a one piece bat. Definitely would have helped for my hands when I played to stop stinging before I went out to pitch.

I need to know this, "is this one for sale?"

He takes the bat from me as we walk back to the counter, "nope this one isn't for sale. The way these bat companies do it is that for a testing model after they decide on what the final design is that's it for the model."

"So this is going to get destroyed after they finalize it?" They can't do that to this one. It still works. It can still do things. Just being destroyed. It didn't even get a chance to play.

Gliding the bat behind the shelf, "probably not but it just won't be used. It's probably just going to be locked back in the storage because we only put out bats for hitting that you could purchase from us."

"It's perfectly good why can't it be used? It can't hit homeruns but it's good at making contact."

"It's more of a free trial before you purchase it from us. We don't want you to make a bad purchase and end up with a bat you don't like."

I might not be able to use this bat again. This bat might not be used for the purposes it was made for, what it wants to be used for. Just a piece that is made for a purpose and that's it.

I plead, "can't you do me a favor and just let me use it when I come back. I come here pretty often and I like swinging that one." He shakes his head no. My shoulders slouch. I want to use this one still. "Hey I have an idea, if they are using the bat for testing I can be the tester you don't even have to pay me. You can write down any information on the hitting. You can even have me do specialized hitting with the bat and I can write down how well it actually preforms."

He looks at me and blows air out from the bottom part of his lip, "I'll ask my manager when he comes back tomorrow."

Chapter 17

The two professional scouts for Aaron show up in matching shirts. Green long sleeve plaid flannel for the Mabfora Salmonberries, salmonberries shimmering on the sleeves as the scouts walk up the stairs of the bleachers. Twenty-four teams in the league and this is the second group of scouts to come and watch us play. First group was excited about us and started talking to everyone. Why they would tell their competition about a gold mine, I won't understand but if it increases Aaron's draft status I will take it.

Not much I can do today, Aaron said not to help and doesn't want my help. If I just tried shouting now he might tattle, quit, and get mad. Just have to wait and enjoy the game. Have to watch a game where he strikes out every single time or walks if a guy can't throw a strike which honestly is unlikely at varsity level.

"Play ball," the umpire says as the home team takes the field. The forecast for today is errors at first base along with a near certainty of strikeouts on all three at-bats. If you're planning on critiquing players come back on a later date so we can actually prepare for the presentation.

First error followed by a strikeout by Aaron. They start marking their sheets. I watch him walk back to the dugout. No telescope in front, no cones set up. This is going to get bad. Just have as few at-bats as possible. Start watching other players, as the game goes on. One more error third inning. Aaron struggling. Fourth inning Aaron first batter warm-ups about to finish.

Am I going to give up on Aaron? I can't give up on him. He needs this. We need this. The gatekeepers, the baseball scouts, the ones judging him on what they see and don't see on the field. They need to see him be a superstar. They see that through statistics, through his ability when they are here, when they are in their office looking at reports and hypothetical analysis of games.

Ball. At least he has some plate discipline even though that ball was in the dirt. Swinging strike, building confidence against Aaron after one strikeout has already happened. Turn towards the scouts as they disapprove. Strike two looking good pitch to hit. Ball as they try getting him to chase. 2-2 just get a walk maybe. Swing and a miss strike three as they go around the horn with the ball.

I look back towards the scouts, the one in the brighter salmonberry shirt says, "he can't play, we're done here. Tell Jason with the Murkers to save the gas for his trip." Oh man, they are ending their thoughts here off the two at-bats. The bleachers clack as they slowly go down the steps.

My mom scoots out of the way as I get out of the bleachers and start to follow them to the parking lot. What can I say to get them to come back next time to watch the game? Make something up. Can't tell them we are cheating.

Past the edge of the building and out of earshot of anyone on the field and anyone on campus no one that can hear this except the scouts. "Aaron's doing terrible today because he broke up with his girlfriend."

The scouts turn around, thank goodness they kinda believe it. Have to be as realistic as possible. He doesn't even have a girlfriend. He hangs out in the chemistry lab by himself not even with the other guys on the baseball team.

They walk towards me wanting more information, "he broke up with his girlfriend today and has been super-bummed out and can't concentrate on anything." There is a reason why he is bad today.

"That is a hit on the intangibles then, but who are you exactly?" the younger one asks.

"I'm his brother, he tells me everything. Didn't tell our parents about his girlfriend though, was actually planning on introducing her to our parents at the game today." Younger one has their eyes wide open, "yeah she broke up with him during lunch period after almost six months of dating. Loved this girl like crazy and the breakup was a total mess." No noise out in the open way. Thank goodness I won't be starting a rumor about Aaron at this school that he will have to deal with.

The one with the salmonberry bush near the top of his shirt asks, "if we draft this guy will this girlfriend cause Aaron problems like this again?"

"What! Huh? No," they look surprised. Have to maintain the story, "she broke up with him, bad break up, no way they are getting back together again. I guarantee it. It was that bad, which is why he is an utter mess. I do think based on how bad it was that he is keeping it together as well as he can on the field right now."

They look towards each other and whisper, this may be a common occurrence in scouting that they have to worry about.

"Aight. We'll comeback next time but he better be able to shrug off devastation or else he'd never survive a cold streak in baseball."

"Don't worry I'm gonna take him to have some fun after the game, make him forget about her. I'm not even gonna mention her name because I want him to forget her." She doesn't even have a name because she doesn't exist.

I walk a little closer, "but in all seriousness though, do me a favor, come back for our next game three days from now. And so, yeah, um, hey, this will probably worry Aaron more than your scouting, but if you end up talking to our parents, don't ever mention the girl cause they don't even know about it."

The younger scout just shakes his head and the brighter salmonberry shirt scout opens his phone and makes a call.

Chapter 18

"Oh man there he is," the pitcher in the bullpen says to the sidearmer next to him.

"The kid whose hitting everything, Aaron Basic? Aaron Base. Yeah Aaron Base is his name. Lucky I am not starting today there goes your ERA," he says right back as he whips his arm to the right. Slider.

"Wait?" I ask standing by the edge of the bullpen seeing the pitches. "How do you know it's him?" I know word is getting around the league like crazy because of his hitting, but how can they know it's him. Is it because of me? He only has had one bad day all season but that isn't slowing the spread of the news about him. Only if he keeps doing bad will it stop. If I can't convince him to take the signs today, it will stop by the end of the month.

"He's the only kid in the league with that kind of bat." The curveball slider combo pitcher says pointing at the edges of eyes popping over the outfield fence.

The edges of the eyes of the bat held in Aaron's backpack go right above the outfield fence as members of the baseball team walk around left field towards the opposing dugout. The reflection of the Letters ICU goes above the fence seeing the entire field.

They noticed him just from his baseball equipment. Not from how he looks but his equipment. They know how well he is doing, demolishing pitching staffs left and right. Save for last game he has been unstoppable. When they see the letters ICU they know that they are in for a world of pain that day.

His ability made everyone wonder who is he, how can we stop him? Can we stop him? Finding any loophole memorizing his equipment. His batting gloves, His bat any exploitable flaws there, none. A brand and message itself, saying when ICU is here Aaron Base is here.

"Want to be the opener for the day? I can come in after the first inning," the just under six foot pitcher says to the side armer as he finishes a throw in the dirt.

"Just so you don't have to face Aaron Base during an at-bat? No way. Just keeping the ball in the ballpark against him is a win."

A few more pitches from both of them as I watch a few more players from our team go into the dugout. The last of the away team must be here. Typically the team caravans in the school bus or with a few parents to an opposing game. Saves gas and is supposed to build team spirit.

Their catchers wave them towards their dugout as they give the space to Sean and our starting pitcher. At most fields they have a bullpen for an away team but at East Starlake High School they only have one and that forces them to share. When I pitched here last year, I kept telling Sean that we need to warm up by our dugout but he said never to do pitching motions on flat surfaces, it messes with your mechanics.

Sean is jogging towards the bullpen as the starter is switching into his cleats. His black hair clumping as he puts his mask over his head as he runs.

"You're being even more brazen John," he says pointing towards the telescope above the outfield fence wall.

"All that matters now is if you are going to do something about it Sean," I say as I look towards the telescope placed above the centerfield wall.

He shakes his head at me and looks downward as the starter runs up with his cleats on. Ultimately rules against cheating in sports are only as good as willingness to enforce them. If there is a rule against cheating in sports, then it's not allowed but if no one actually gets in trouble for breaking the rule then is there really a rule in the first place? And that only matters if you get caught. Because how can you get punished if no one even knows your cheating?

The green grass crumples as I walk towards the bleachers. Got here early and set the telescope up even without Aaron agreeing yes. There is no way that he couldn't have seen it walking in here. Have to go convince Aaron as soon as I can, those scouts won't be patient forever. You have to be consistent. In their eyes you have to be able to bounce back from anything.

Bleachers creek as I pass the front rows of scouts and sit next to Mom and Dad. More scouts showed up this time. The scouts from the Salmonberries are here again along with a few more sets of scouts. Most important game once again. The most important game will always be the one you are playing in right now because that is the only for sure game you actually have.

Away team takes their part of the outfield to warm-up as Aaron stands in the back following the stretches given. Scouts keeping their notebooks open ready for what happens. Is he able to bounce back? Was it just a really good hot streak? Should we invest our limited baseball resources into him?

Warm-up throws as they prep for the game. Basic sprints and shuffles preparing to play. Coach signals for infield to go towards the dugout to get some grounders by the dugout as he hits some flyballs to the outfielders. Run towards the dugout. I need to talk to Aaron and convince him now. A light creek from the bleachers on my last step down as I move to stand towards the dugout.

Aaron standing in-line to take grounders from the first base coach. Ball goes by the first fielder. Next person goes by also. You're hitting it too hard coach. Don't try and impress scouts. You're past your time playing too. Next fielder gets it off a quick grab. Lucky there. Ball rolled back and Aaron is up.

Takes two steps back but coach tells him to move closer. I boo the coach and tell him to be realistic with his hitting. They are way too close to him at that speed. Sharp hit towards Aaron and one hop and it gets Aaron in the shin. Ball rolls towards the mound as Aaron hops up and down on one foot in pain. I shake my head at the coach and lean over the fence, "Come on coach ease up. Put me in to hit."

I think I got the coach mad. He signals for the team to sit on the bench until the game starts, only a few minutes until game time. Is he going to talk to me, what can he do now? Bench me I can't even play anymore. He can't eject me, he isn't an umpire. When you're actually on the team, you have to follow the coaches no matter how incompetent they are. A lot of the times the coaches know less than the players, know less strategy, but we have to respect them because they are older adults. But just because you're the coach doesn't mean you know what you are doing.

Aaron step hops towards the side of the dugout where his bat equipment is while the coach picks up the ball from the mound and then walks towards the head coach. They can't kick me out, only the umpire can do that. And most umpires don't even like the coaches.

Just on the edge of the dugout I wave Aaron to scoot over so I can talk to him.

"You ok there champ?"

"Yeah," he says rubbing his shin. "Probably going to be a bruise."

"That coach doesn't know what he's doing," I say and Aaron looks at me questionly. "What's that coach gonna do? Take me out the lineup, he can't do that anymore." I shake my head and look towards the first base coach talking to the manager, "he is just trying to gloat and make you miss and try lowering your guys' self esteem cause you miss. People can't react to a ball in that short amount of time."

Aaron points towards centerfield, "I saw the telescope again that you placed before we got here."

I try and keep my voice down so no one hears in the dugout. Most of the team is trying to get mentally set for the game. No one sitting near us but I can't risk anyone accidentally hearing. "I put it there because I am looking out for you Aaron that's the only way I know how."

Aaron looks at his ICU bat, its eyes glaring at me and the telescope in the outfield, "what about the other people that are victims of this scheme you did? Zack left the team because of me."

"Yeah I know Zack quit and that is it for his baseball career. But I am not looking out for them, I am looking out after you because you are my brother. Getting you to become a professional for an even brief moment in your life will protect the rest of it for as long as you live."

"But he cared about the sport more than I do, everyone else here does." A few more hits towards the outfield, easy flies where they deal with the gentle wind. Other team taking their outfield warm-ups on the other side about to go back into the dugout.

"I'll be honest with you right now Aaron. Most kids at the end of high school, that is it for sports. Ending or damaging it for them now is ending it just a little early. And I know that's tragic that kids can't play anymore. But most kids don't have the dream to become a professional baseball player. But there is a whole lot more money in sports than almost anything."

"But you already know I don't want to be a professional player. You do," Aaron says to me. Fielders coming in from the outfield.

"You're not upset because of cheating." I take a step back, "you're upset because your damaging the potential for other guys. Would you still be upset if you actually were any good?"

“Probably would.” My brother Aaron Base, not really competitive at all.

Coaches start to come into the dugout last time I can say anything before someone definitely hears, “in anything you do you ultimately are going to be competing with someone else. There is only a limited number of spots available anywhere. When you are good or at least you are able to be good, you are going to be knocking down some others that can’t keep up. I know you don’t like it but that just is what happens.”

Aaron looks down at the concrete dugout, “Ok I’ll do it. But I don’t want to. You're the one making me do this, remember that.” He gets his batting gloves on his hands looking towards the outfield.

Fist bump Aaron that he rejects and I go back as the home team takes the field. Umpires talking and getting set. Nothing I can do now but sit back and get ready for some action from Aaron Base.

Umpire signals to start the game as the balls come in and the pitcher gets set. Randy up first looking towards third at the third baseman and the manager. No bunt sign. Fastball low and away. One finger down, away from Randy. Takes the first pitch. Fastball for a strike Good.

I can’t have only two pitches seen. before I can signal to Aaron. What’s the pitch order? Some pitchers choose to have their curveball as number two instead of a change-up. Others have a different breaking pitch in that spot. This guy throwing a fastball change-up curveball slider means four pitches in almost every order.

Two fingers down once again outside part of the plate. Ok after this pitch I have half the possible pitches down. Ball coming in straight no bend. One one that must mean it is a change-up. It can’t be a fastball because it looked like the same pitch. Could have it been a mispitch? No, unlikely. Probably not much difference with his fastball change-up, probably not his best pitch. Maybe just checking to see what is working.

Back to one finger inside part of the plate. Fastball inside. Grounder towards shortstop and a thrown out. Run back across the infield towards the dugout. That was an ok at-bat but it could have been better but I will take it. Sean will give us the other pitch.

Sean up and three fingers right over the middle of the plate glove going low. It’s going to be a curveball. Pitcher lifts his leg and the ball sails right over the plate bending like a curveball should. That means slider is number four. If there are only four possible pitches and you know what the first three are, then you really know signal four because the last possible pitch will be the sign you haven't seen yet.

Four fingers down away right on the corner. Pitch coming and just on the edge for a strike. Off speed seems to be working on those pitches, nothing that Aaron can't handle so long as we go through with this.

Two strikes, Fastball signaled for way above the strike zone. Don't swing. And he swings three strikes and he is back to the dugout as Aaron goes to take his turn with everyone watching. Very important at-bat. Ball goes around the horn and the sidearmer at first base walks the ball back towards the pitcher and lets him get ready for the big man up to bat.

Another upside to knowing what pitch it is that me and Aaron haven't really used is that you know when not to actually swing at a pitch. Sometimes people will set up a pitch purposely for a ball, honestly it doesn't make much sense at all. It wastes pitcher's energy, sets him off his rhythm if he is throwing strikes and it can mess with an umpire's strike zone that he sets up in his mind. The idea is that the hitter will swing at a ball but that rarely ever happens, so you should just be throwing strikes as much as you can. But as a hitter I will take a free ball any day.

"Put your phone down he's up for the first time today," my mom says. "Get a base hit Aaron."

Here is the time to leave an impression on these scouts, "make some solid contact now!" Fastball outside strike one. Aaron steps out of the box and takes a gentle practice swing rolls his shoulders back right in. Is he changing his mind again? I can know the mind of the catcher and pitcher but I cannot know the mind of my own brother. Three fingers down curveball inside, "Wait for your pitch if you have to Aaron."

"Well he waited for his pitch now it's two strikes," my mom glares at me. Shouting back at Aaron, "don't strike out, protect the plate and fight off the bad pitch if you have to!"

Fastball no, change-up outside part of the plate yes. I would have gone with a fastball in this case. He took the pitch earlier. "Let's go Aaron!" Pitcher takes a deep breath in and starts his motion. What will keep Aaron's career going for just a little while longer down to this pitch. Take the pitch and it's a strike then it's over. The scouts will walk away. A hit keeps it going for a little while longer.

Ball one off the plate a few inches. I exhale and blow air out my lips. Good take but at two strikes you put yourself at the whims of an umpire that might make the strike zone a little bigger. Fastball outside part of the plate probably don't want to let him turn on the pitch, "make some solid contact now!"

Scouts eyes on Aaron. ICU bat eyes on me. Me watching the screen. Pitcher briefly closes his eyes then reopens them for the pitch. From the windup the pitch leaves his hand.

Bat bolts through the strike zone. Ball hits the U of the bat and speeds high into the outfield. Get out of here get out of here. Ball starting to die. Get out of here please. Left fielder going back looking at the wall judging it jumps and it's just past the fence. Homerun Aaron Base!

He listened to the signals I gave. Kids walk out of the dugout as he trots past first base. Scouts talk amongst each other about Aaron Base. Ok he is a legitimate player. He can play, might have a few emotional issues but just keep an eye on him and he should be fine. Batting results good this year so far. Definitely a draft pick what order will matter later but we know what he can do. John and Aaron Base are back in this. Aaron Base all the ability and decisions for Aaron Base.

But there is no John Base. Just Aaron Base. No share of the glory to the public. No ability to do that. But maybe there is a way to actually get that same respect from the glory?

The pitcher shakes his head at his first baseman, looks like we didn't keep the ball in the ballpark this time. Aaron rounds third as Sean grabs the ICU bat and walks it towards the dugout. Ignoring the celebration but only came out because everyone else made him to.

Those two pitchers remembered him from his bat alone.

I need to get a bat myself. That Pawn Bat can't be used anymore but it can be used for something. They remembered Aaron when he came with the ICU bat maybe they will recognize me with the PAWN bat. Brother of Aaron Base, when he is there Aaron will be there to.

Chapter 19

I glide the Pawn bat along the chainlink fence rattling the bat against the bullpen area. Cody, the backup left fielder with Charisma City before the borders changed, now starting pitcher for East Charisma City High School is getting ready for the game. Back in the system, Aaron at least willing to participate, time to leave my mark before the game. The batting cages said to let them know weekly how the Pawn bat does and how effective it is outside the cages. Aaron says it's too small for him to use but it can be effective in other ways.

"You guys getting ready to take a loss today?" I say as I park the bat on top of my shoulder.

"Oh hey John," Cody says as he continues a lightbulb stretch. "I thought you graduated last year?"

"I did, but I'm here to watch my brother deliver a homerun beatdown today," I remark as I lean against the fence.

Cody looks confused, "then what's with the bat? That's not his, his has eyeballs on it."

"It's a message when the pawn shows up Aaron Base is about to arrive on the field," I say as I take a batting stance. Cody shakes his head at me and starts to shift towards palm away from him and then starts to warm up with his catcher.

Did Cody learn any pitches in the offseason? I remember that he was a sinkerballer but did he pick up anything like a cutter or a split finger over the break? First throw and he windmills his arm after the release. Sinker again.

Stretching is actually really important for pitching. Even though it looks just like you're throwing a baseball it actually is a lot harder and more painful than it looks. Your arm to throw a baseball that fast has to go just as fast as the ball is going. All the force all on the arm produces a lot of pressure on the tendons and joints. Stretching can help make your body be a little more ready for the damage it's going to take while your pitching. Some people say you have to pitch without stretching and be ready at any moment but I personally think that is dangerous to actually do that. Very easy to get hurt doing that.

"So is Aaron going to go and use that Pawn bat and is switching out the ICU?" he asks as he motions for another pitch. Sinker again. No new pitches most likely.

"Nope, I've got it ready for him if he ever wants it though. Always standing by ready for a couple of hacks to take a swing. It will always be there in the stands for him."

"Wait, then why doesn't he just have it then?" Cody's jaw drops and he takes a step off the mound towards the edge of the bullpen. "Oh man," he waves off his catcher and motions for him to get some water from the warming sun. "You're bringing that bat over here because you want to be in the game. You're trying to help Aaron."

My stomach pinches. Is he realizing the sign stealing? Helping Aaron through all the games since he has gotten back on board with the codes.

"You're not going to intimidate me or anyone John no matter how hard you try. Want to know why, you're not playing anymore. That Pawn bat isn't doing anything, just sitting on your shoulder."

I brush him off, "you're just nervous you're going up against Aaron Base."

He waves off his catcher again who wants him to refocus. "Am I nervous about pitching against Aaron? Of course I am. Guy like that is doing amazing. But am I nervous about you showing up with that Pawn bat to intimidate me about Aaron Base? Not in the slightest. You're not even playing. You are not Aaron Base."

"But I always am here before Aaron shows up." Worked on this since last night, "The pawn always goes before the King." Cody puts his head in his glove. Ok not what I expected. "But yeah if I am here Aaron Base will be here."

"Yeah you're his brother, who else would you be watching?"

"And doesn't that at least intimidate you a bit?" I say as I roll my right shoulder with the bat on the edge of the bone.

Cody putting two and two together as he shakes his head. If John Base shows up then Aaron will be there. Shouldn't that at least be intimidating some pitchers? The other guys were intimidated by Aaron.

"You're being really ridiculous you honestly won't make a single player in this league nervous. Aaron might but you aren't even playing anymore." The catcher really wants him to get back to warming up, Cody sees and continues talking anyways, "but seriously John, you can't live your life through Aaron. You can maybe be his cheerleader all you want but you aren't making anyone nervous by just showing up. You're not part of the game anymore." I see one or two more kids from the team emerge from the locker rooms, uniforms ready and clean for the game. "We played for a few years together and I loved every second of it, but here is the thing, you have to move on from baseball. You can't be living baseball through your brother. I know he is doing great and honestly is probably the best hitter I've ever seen, but you need to move on from this. I'm graduating this year and this year probably is the last time I'm pitching too but I'm making peace with it every time I'm on the mound."

He motions again to his catch for one more second, "John, you can be his favorite little spectator all you want but it won't scare anyone, it won't make anyone play worse than if you didn't show up. I'm saying this as your friend. You need to move on. You can't try living through your brother. I know he is doing great, and honestly is a better player than you, but you need to move on from this. I'm graduating this year and a whole lot of stuff is ending for me too, even baseball, but I am accepting in and enjoying it while I can." He turns as he goes back towards throwing his pitches.

Cody is just nervous that he is going to get demolished by Aaron. I will eventually intimidate someone and help Aaron. When I show up it means Aaron Base is coming. Someone will see that I am apart of his greatness not just unknowable. I will bring this bat to every game if I have to and park it in the stands bring it to the bullpens and remind everyone Aaron Base is coming. John Base is still here. At least one person will remember that I helped Aaron Base even a little.

I check the telescope through my phone and it is aimed right where it needs to be.

Chapter 20

Multiple apps open same time. Aaron on deck. Manage every path at once. On the phone with the batting coach of the Palm Bush Sand Dabs. Mom and Dad have given me just a tad of space when I am on the phone. Got to be quick to watch my screen when I need to and hide the text messages from the Spencestead Murkers and the Colmon City Wall Bouncers. Both of those teams have been on the news recently, reports on their actions preparing for the draft. Trade for the first round first pick. Buy the rights to the second first round pick if the first rounder gets a pitcher. There was even talk of a few teams thinking of tanking to get the first round pick for Aaron. All so that they have the chance to sign Aaron Base.

Officially became Aaron's licensed agent two weeks ago. Filled out the forms with the government to be his agent. Thankfully, we live in an area were the requirements to be a sports agent are limited, other areas require you to have a law degree, others have you meet certain years of negotiation experience. I have to do a few online courses with the government to meet the requirements here but I have almost a year to do them. In the mean time they are letting me operate so long as I have less than five clients and take less than ten percent of their wages for my services.

Aaron at bat runner at third. "Let's go Aaron." Sand Dabs' batting coach wants to know about Aaron's bat speed ratio. Spencestead Murkers are seeing if they can trade draft picks and what is Aaron's minimum salary.

Unlike most other draft picks where the negotiation is one-sided, I made Aaron so good that it's now two-sided. If the offer is not good enough Aaron could walk away. Normally that would be a death sentence to an athlete, but I can argue to them at the negotiation table that Aaron is so good that foreign teams can sign him as a free agent. Go to college for a year to showcase his ability even further. Even just wait a year for a better chance with the next draft cycle. Sign him but don't pay enough money, we leave. And teams need to see if they have enough money in their pockets to pay for this.

Thirty three million for three years. Signing bonus of eight million.

Thirty-Three Million Dollars. That ties the largest signing for a rookie in the history of the league. The Murkers want Aaron so bad they will offer him that much money for three years of his life. Three years of his life for money that will last lifetimes and generations. People who might not even ever know him will benefit from his money.

Thirty nine million for three years. Signing bonus of nine million. Three million deferred. We want an exit option after the second year.

That is now the highest offer for a rookie signing in the history of the league maybe even history of sports. In a text message to me. Sitting at the end of the bleachers. They are offering him that much money to just hit a baseball. Hardly running around, not tackling people, no kicking people in the head, just going to the plate and making a swing that sends the ball to the outfield. They don't want to risk it all on Aaron. But this makes him the most valued rookie of all time. If he signs, I almost become a millionaire before I am twenty.

"Gotta take command out there Aaron."

I walk down the bleachers towards the backstop, my feet muffling my words to the fans around us, "I just got a bite with the Wall Bouncers for thirty-nine mil for three years. Give me something better Andy that I can tell Aaron after the game."

A sad sigh from the batting coach, "we only have twenty-seven to spend for a first baseman this year. We're a small market team, and we can't have that much of a dent on the payroll."

"Hey, then I saved you a draft pick then. If you got the chance to get us, then skip us cause you can't afford my brother."

A shock over the phone, "oh no we will get what we can. Forty million three years. Signing bonus of eight million. Best I can do. Anything else I'm going to have to get the owner and our general manager on the phone."

"You can give them my number," and the phone disconnects. One-one. Catcher signals backdoor curveball outside, "show them what the ICU can do Aaron." Bang off the sweet spot of the barrel. Ball lining itself towards left field over the left fielder's head and just over the wall and bounces on the street to the front of a neighbor's house. Time for another walk as Aaron trots for his homerun.

With that much money on the line they are definitely calculating worth and risk. Can he bring a championship with their roster? Can he bring multiple? What if he gets injured? Is he willing to stay past his first contract? If he is that good can we trade him to a richer team for more money? Hot potato on a gold mine.

I pass by the concession table that has been present at every home game now for a month. More and more people are showing up and the varsity team has been having a parent selling snacks so they can save up to get new things. New bats. New field tractor. Coach has been trying to remind Aaron when he signs the contract not to forget about the school here.

Gen Manager and Owners said they are willing to give part ownership of the team for him to play for the Sand Dabs.

Owning part of a baseball team. A small one, but they are giving him the last asset they have that is valuable to keep him if they can get him. Baseball once had player-managers. But I never heard of a player-owner. Some teams are valued in the tens of billions of dollars, Aaron isn't getting that much of a share obviously, but he could very well own a baseball team. Getting to watch every game from his luxury box near the top of the stadium, picking the general manager and manager. Finding the next great player, and avoiding the biggest draft-bust.

Walk past the edge of the field and back onto the street. Cars clear as I go pick up the ball. Pristine like new. Red marked seams with maybe Sand Dab white leather? This one is going back to the team as they have lost a good number of balls to the Homeruns from Aaron. Balls that landed in a backyard. Balls that rolled into the gutter. Aaron has gotten to keep some of them to remember the season by. But with so many the team needs to keep something.

Turn around as my phone buzzes in my pocket. Inning over as Aaron runs back out to first base with the crowd cheering for him. I'm just a pawn. Just like my bat I get myself in position to improve the ability of other better pieces to do their job. Other pieces on the board more valuable than me. But sometimes pawns are more valuable than every other piece on the board combined. More valuable that the king who can't move more than one space, the king who can't even play. The king would be nothing without me but I can't do anything by myself either. An all seeing eye that sees every pitcher but yet cannot hit the ball himself.

I check the message on my phone and the proposal breaks the previous record set a few minutes ago.

Chapter 21

The stands start to creak just as five more people go up the stairs of the bleachers. This place has been packed since we turned towards May. A kid that is a near guarantee to get a hit, but not just any hit but a homerun or a double at least, every single at-bat. When he is up you know that he is a threat. Can anyone stop him? Everyone wants to find out. Will he continue the streak of near perfection? Everyone wants to know.

Warm windy day as the spring flowers start to bloom in the eighty degree heat. A few sprinklers across the street of the neighboring houses have been going on and off throughout the day. Made sure that Dad didn't set the sprinklers on during the game or else a few drops can land on the lens and blur the picture.

All it takes is for one thing to go wrong and this all falls apart. Labeled as frauds. Banned from the draft. Reputations destroyed. All because I was stealing baseball signs.

These stands never had this many people when I played. Maybe even more than a basketball game. When I played there never was this many people. They are all here because Aaron is big and can hit. They don't show up to see anyone else. As much as people say you need to hustle or you need to try. You actually don't, you just need to be great. And greatness will be outside the reach of some no matter how hard they hustle and try.

People showed up early this time. I will have to get here earlier for the last few games of the season. "Get a hit now kid!" my voice aches from the top of the bleachers. Don't want to be too far back because Aaron might not be able to hear me over the people no matter how hard I try. When people scream and shout for Aaron when he's up, my voice blends in and can be unhearable. If he can't hear what signs are coming then it doesn't matter if I have the best system set up. He's back to embarrassing himself.

Runner on second, Aaron pops one up behind home plate jutting up with high wind taking it over the bleachers and back towards school buildings. Couple of people still following the ball just as it lands behind us. Next pitch coming. Small wave attempt by the crowd. No one really goes for it. "Drive it the other way Aaron!" He smacks the ball along the left field foul line just landing fair. Crowds eyes go towards the ball Aaron turns the corner around first.

Some brown haired girl is staring at me a few rows down. More like glaring like she realized something. Aaron half way to second coach waving on to third. She points her index and middle fingers at her chest then both her eyes and lasers her fingers at me. Puts both her hands in a cup shape and pretends to look at a phone. I see you. The ICU bat rolls on the ground, eyes seeing me. Ball coming in towards third Aaron slides. Out at third base.

She knows and we just got caught. She waves me down towards the concession stand as she gets out of her seat. How did she figure it out? Now there is another person. Sean knows, she knows. Who is she going to tell about this? Oh man, my stomach sinks. I have to talk to her, know what she wants. Not much of a choice. Just remain as calm as possible.

Step down off the end of the bleachers and towards the concession stand. Just buy something small or pretend to browse the few candies they have there.

In the process of buying herself a candy bar, "must be an amazing sight to see Aaron Base hitting that way everyday." She is being vague on purpose, not wanting to alert the concession stand parent.

"What did you actually see?" my mind begs for an answer.

"Strange you don't remember me, oh well that's fine," she pays for her candy bar. "At first I thought I saw some sign stealing out there on the field," she pauses and looks at me. Is this the same girl who was stealing plays earlier? I think it is. "But then I thought, sign stealing? That doesn't make any sense. I looked around again and all I saw was some kid that was too preoccupied with his phone to be watching a baseball game."

She knows but won't say. If she says I'm sign stealing, I will just say she was play stealing. I don't know who she is but I could probably figure it out, other kids in the gym at the time would probably recognize her. Losing her school's championship banner. Aaron losing his draft pick. Nothing to gain over one game. I don't know if her brother is playing, but even if he is the pitcher, he only has to face Aaron at most twice. It's better for her to keep quiet.

"Hmm strange, just like stealing basketball plays, doesn't make any sense." I start to look at the candy bar selection. Just go with a chocolate. She walks back to her seat.

Every moment wondering if it is the end and someone realizes what happened. One action by someone else determining the fate of my life. If this works I can become very rich. If not that avenue in life closed forever. Every time Aaron goes to bat, a risk of being discovered. Every single at-bat having a potential outcome of the career ending.

Take a bite of the candy bar and it tastes sour. Shouldn't have bought it but I needed to blend in. Take the steps back to my seat. Full rows where once I could sit wherever I want, now I have to save a seat. All because of Aaron Base. Not for the team but to watch Aaron Base and to see history in the making. The next best baseball player of the generation while he is just emerging.

Everyone loves Aaron but the only thing that can happen for me is that they hate me. At best no one will know who I am because they never discover the scheme. Just Aaron Base's brother, but if the public finds out they will hate me. There is no other way the public will ever know about me. Head of a scheme that fooled the baseball league and the world. But if they don't find out then I am just the brother of a draft-bust. Brother of someone forgotten in the league after a few years and remembered only in articles online about baseball history. Empty seats for me but a full crowd for Aaron.

I look at the bat that is holding my seat and see the name. Pawn. Just a tool for me to get a spot. Not being used for what it wants to be used for. Just a tool to be used to support a superstar. Known by the title of his job and nothing else. Left in the dust while people cheer for the superstar.

Chapter 22

Aaron dawns the catcher's gear just as the May sun goes overhead. Senior day. Don't embarrass yourself too much. The one day when seniors get to play any spot they want to. Typically it's the happiest day for seniors who don't play much. If you stuck it out in your senior year as a bench warmer or someone took your spot in the middle of senior year this is your last time to play. If that guy, Zack ended up staying on the team he would probably be holding first base while Aaron would be catching.

A lefty catcher, please don't hurt the batters Aaron. Thank goodness I never caught, all that gear just seems so heavy and having to crouch down the entire game just looks exhausting. Balls in coming down. Leaps up and throws a missile right over Eric's head caught by Markie before it goes into the outfield. Don't steal off of him please, unless you're slow and then maybe if Aaron gets a good throw to second.

Righty up to the plate, his clean white and green uniform catches just a little bit of the breeze. Do not hit the batter on the throw back to the pitcher. You're being judged by how well you hit and how you barely manage first base, don't be making it any harder by showing that you can't catch either. I know that you're not even going to be a catcher, but this can only go bad if you hit the batter in the head as you throw a pitch back to the hurler. Or let another past ball go by you.

One ball no strikes. Line drive up the middle. I wonder what exactly a catcher sees when the ball gets hit, does he see the ball leave the bat immediately? Can he tell if a swing is going to miss before it does? Does he know a ball is a homerun the moment it leaves the bat?

Next batter comes to the plate as the runner takes his lead. Gentle blowing of the grass as the crowd maintains its good size through the fifth inning. Ever since Aaron has been doing so well even more people are showing up, just to watch him. Not just scouts but students and staff from the school and occasionally local residents who want to see some homerun magic. Bleachers and sides completely full.

Foul tip to the head. That's got to hurt. I'm actually surprised Sean never complained on any pitches that actually hit him on a foul tip. Aaron takes a moment to collect himself calling time to the umpire as he picks up the ball. Sean probably deals with that so much. Sitting on the bench on as

Aaron enjoys his senior day and next year Sean will have his. Just watching Aaron biding his time.

Groundball to Eric going towards second. Scooped and flips to second. Out throws to first, ball touches the dirt as the first baseman tries and gets the scoop. Second out. Aaron should have been running behind the runner to get a ball that gets by the first baseman. Even though the foul area is small a ball that gets by the first baseman could for an average runner get an extra base. Catching is a lot more than just sitting behind the dish, you have to move on every play. Every position should always be moving on each play.

Strike one and the throw back is a wild throw. I shake my head as Eric has to get the ball from Randy in center. Bottom of the lineup good chance that this is the last batter of the inning. Strike two. Just don't have the ball go by you Aaron on the next strike and you can get out of catching. Don't try going another inning of this. Ball one. Passed ball. I could have caught that.

I take steps down the bleachers passing full rows, inning about to be over. I should check to see how Aaron is feeling after that foul ball to the head. Some people think that baseball is a non-exercising sport but that is really only for a few positions like maybe first base and designated hitter if your league has it. You might run a little bit and that's it in the whole game. But positions like pitcher and catcher are positions where you actually work out playing. Every ball the pitcher throws the catcher throws straight back.

Walking behind the dugout to hear the umpire shout strike three and the inning is over. The brief foray into catching is done. Just one inning at catcher after trying his luck at pitching and quickly getting pulled after beaming the first two batters. Aaron's metal cleats clack as they shift from the infield dirt to the concrete dugout. He's first one in as everyone else is jogging back towards the dugout.

"Tough to actually play baseball when there isn't anyone to help you," Sean says to Aaron just as he sits down in the corner towards the edge. Unsnap one leg guard top to bottom. Put it in Sean's spot just as Sean walks away towards the door of the dugout not wanting to deal with it.

“I’m actually surprised that no one figured it out,” Aaron says to me as he unstraps the back of the chest protector. I look towards the outfield at the camera remembering the conversation that Sean told me earlier. Stop cheating. At least we won’t be cheating anymore in two weeks. Two away games and the final home game.

“You could see it from behind home plate but just barely, blends in perfectly so you wouldn’t notice, but after all day you’d probably think that it looks weird.”

I never told Aaron about Sean coming over to the store and Sean talking to me. Aaron would probably get really nervous if I told him. He’d say we would have to tell everyone what we did. Every single person would figure out we kept this going for months. We would have wasted our time. Aaron would have been sitting on the bench. He might have even quit mid-year sitting on the bench doing nothing. No more baseball for either of us. I wouldn’t have been watching any games. All the people in the crowd that weren’t there before wouldn’t have been there now.

“Don’t worry no one is drafting you for your catching, they are going for your ability to hit. Nothing is going to happen,” I respond as Sean glares at me and keeps his mouth quiet from telling the coach. The eyes of the ICU bat next to Aaron glare back at me too.

Chapter 23

Seven different scouts emailed me and called me at work to say they were going to see the final away game. They are going through a regional trip and watching this game before going to watch the Southwest Regional High School Baseball Championship. Some other prospects are playing there and they can't miss that one. They will have this one last time to see Aaron to make their final judgements. I don't think any scouts are seeing the last game at home, just fans and people ready to see the final game of the year. Final game of baseball for so many people.

I walk with the bulky janitor up the second floor stairs to the roof of the building that acts as the center field wall. Three thirty to right three forty to left three fifty to center but a forty-five foot building acting as a fourth outfielder behind the centerfielder. A gentle curvy building where the classrooms below have a relaxing view of the field and the small trees behind the bleachers.

The door to the roof opens as I get a great view of the May sky, and green baseball field. Tractor finishing setting up the infield. Slight amount of trees offering shade to parts of the stands behind home plate. They are ready for their last game.

"I'm just gonna leave this here while I record the game, I'll be back before you have to go home," I tell him. Spread out the equipment and set up the box for the platform.

He takes a look at the telescope, "Ooo I used to play football and thinking about it, this could be a perfect way for someone to steal the plays from the high school team here. Having a camera in a hidden place and I'm surprised no one has decided on recording practices for the teams they have to play against the week before."

Oh man don't have him get any ideas. Thank goodness he doesn't play baseball. Former lineman based on his size. You could cheat in just about every sport with technology. Sports were made in times before all this new technology. Even the more modern e-sports can be cheated with different types of technology. Exploits in the game that you can find if you look deep in the rules, deep in the code. With tech in the physical space, sports are now in open season and everything we hold dear there is being hunted into oblivion.

"I heard that kinda stuff happens in basketball games all the time. You gotta keep your plays secret in that game," I say to him, just keep him off of baseball.

"Wow I totally have to tell the athletic director about that, probably make me set up a metal detector in the lobby of the gym," he says just as he points for us to get off the roof. You can tell the director that. Aaron won't be a high schooler next week and I'm not into cheating in basketball. But there are some people who are.

The janitor grabs the rest of his equipment and walks into a classroom on the second floor. Hard to believe that I was in one of these one year ago. Pass by posters for graduation, prom, and other end of year festivities. Turn corner and see cabinet of school trophies. Wrestling, Football and the rest. I wonder if that janitor ever won a trophy for his school.

Exit out of the brick building out onto the grass along the right field fence of the baseball field. Green wall non-see through. Check the camera presets clear. At least I used high school math for something. Games of angles for telescope will soon transition to games of statistics for the professional baseball draft. Increase the probability of high quality draft contracts by highlighting Aaron's ability. Show that Aaron could walk away to be able to demand more value.

Turn the corner on the right field fence and see foldable chairs by the start of the bullpen all the way towards the backstop and around the other side. Lots of people here to see everything going on. Final game of the year for this team. Our last away game. I see my parents have saved my seat second row behind home plate, or at least my Pawn bat has saved the seat for me. Even though Aaron hasn't used it in a game sticking with the ICU, I still keep it if he ever needs it though it only once intimidated one pitcher in the whole season. I guess I legitimately helped out with two at-bats with the Pawn bat in my career. That's what I told the batting cages at least.

Take my seat just as the first pitch is thrown. Need to showcase power to blow them away. Told Aaron that it would be great to get one over the building in center field. Janitor said I can go up there to get any baseballs. Getting it over the wall in center is going to showcase real power to the scouts. There will be no doubt left that he will constantly be hitting homeruns anywhere. Fields that are beyond five hundred feet to center. Fields that have even higher walls in the outfield. Games played at below sea level. One time over center field means that the stadium cannot stop you.

Randy at second base one out Aaron is up. Slider outside corner, “Drive it the other way Aaron.”

“What are you talking about?” My mom looks at me, “he should be trying to pull the ball, get the runner over to third base.”

One ball no strikes same pitch again. Mom is going to say something. “Drive it the other way Aaron.” Mom glares at me, “put down the phone and stop giving Aaron bad advice.”

That’s what the pitcher actually wants, a ball to the left side of the field with a runner on second makes it more likely he can’t advance to third. Grounder to third or short, just check the runner back to second and get the out at first. Ball to the left fielder, has a chance to get you out at third base if you over run the bag and he’s quick.

I keep my phone open and the count is one and one. Change-up outside. Thank goodness the words make sense on this pitch, “let’s go Aaron.” Pitcher checks runner at second, pitch coming. Smack. The ball goes right back up the middle and rockets on a hop to the center fielder. Randy holds up at third base.

Ok base hit. Just a single but that would have been a double if he hit that ball into the gap. They tell kids to try and hit the ball back up the middle, but that is just going to get a single. The center fielder is going to get the ball and he is pretty close to second base, easy out at second if you try for it. If there is a runner in scoring position on second a liner into center field tests the center fielder’s arm. The thing is center usually is running in on those plays since he is getting a ball on a hop from the liner. Good chance of getting out at home. Swing the ball in the gap however, he’s not running in, anyway he goes he’s not going straight towards second base or home. Double maybe a triple if it goes by the three guys in the outfield.

First and third catcher signals to his team. Don’t give Aaron the steal sign coach. Have him stay back and wait for a big hit to bring him in. We tried stealing off the pitcher signs once or twice in the year. It worked each time but it was close. After those times I stopped shouting towards first base whether or not to steal a base. Pitcher goes for a change-up trying to get a double play. Not gonna give Aaron the steal signal. Grounder up the middle. Aaron going for third. Don't run you're too slow stay back. Run scores throw to third. Dead in the water and Aaron slows up letting himself be tagged. That is taking about forty thousand off the signing bonus.

Aaron why don't any of the scouts see through this? You don't know how to run on the basepaths. You can't field. Only thing you're good at is hitting. Maybe they might designated hitter you, but can you possibly be any worse at this sport? Maybe it's because you're too good to actually be true and they think this is your flaw. Bad fielding and base running.

Half inning the whole inning over. Next inning they tie the game up. Top of the third Aaron up again. Randy at third base time for a homerun.

Fastball outside up, "gotta take command out there Aaron" Swing at the first pitch. Disappears off the bat and reappears in deep center. Going and bounces against almost the top of the building back towards the field of play. Almost had it. Could look bad that it didn't go over. Still have some more time. Double as he is held up at second base standing up.

The gentle curve of the building ensures there are no crazy bounces off the wall that could possibly confuse an outfielder, even if he takes a bad route on the ball. Thank goodness Aaron won't have to ever have to run to get a ball that the right fielder might misjudge. No way that will happen off this fourth outfielder. Ball will bounce straight and true off the wall back towards the field of play as it's just a gentle smooth angle.

Few of Aaron's hits are actually close at second base or anywhere really. Usually he has been just trotting up to second or trotting around the bases. No sprinting, no running really. Easy quick motion like lifting a weight at the gym. Big weight but once and done.

Top six and Aaron is up for probably his last time today. Just get a homerun in center and that will be my excuse to go leave and get the ball and disassemble the telescope. Come on signal something good. No one on base, too bad we can't show how unmovable Aaron is under pressure now. Some choke under the pressure, but the all seeing eye of the bat doesn't see anything different when the game is on the line or not.

Fastball outside. Strike. Fastball outside. Ball. Backdoor curveball gets signaled. Easily crushed to center and lined on top of the roof. The fourth outfielder no match for the power of the all seeing eye. The all seeing eye with omnipotence of a baseball swing, if that skill could be taken to the professional league, Aaron would be the ruler over all of baseball. Everyone else kneeling at his throne.

I walk down towards the visitor's dugout as Aaron goes and puts his bat right back in its spot. The dew on the grass covering the bottom of the eyes as if they are crying for what has just happened. Tears of joy for the excellent season. Tears of sadness that it's over. Tears of hate for them being used for this. I'll never know, so many emotions clouded among this whole scheme coming to an end. Or at least part of it. The next part is the image prep for the draft.

Open the door to the school building and see a copper statue of the founder. Strong dignified, no gum or scratches on it. Need to make him the idealized image of what we need him to be. Get sponsorships for clothing, image approval. I'm sure this founder here has done one or two things that are bad but people tend to forget that when you have a statue or school named after you. The way you keep an image that you want is by putting positive elements towards it. Schools and statues are nice.

Go up the stairs to the second floor as I see a few teachers grading students papers. Lots of assignments lots of hopes depending on the finals tomorrow. Final exams determining colleges, classes for next year. A whole lot riding on the work that they did over the semester.

No one followed me towards the roof. Pass into the dark corridor and walk up the angle for the roof access. Locked. I push the door again. It won't budge. Oh no. Pull the door won't move. Oh no! It's locked. I rush back down the walkway into the halls to find the janitor. Should I ask a teacher? No, then they are going to ask why. Janitor doesn't know anything but one of them might. I sprint through the hall my feet clacking the sound down the corridor and back again. Where is he? Where is he?!

Left right not inside the second floor. I rush down the stairs to check the rest of the building and any map of the school. Too many buildings on this campus. Some past left field, others beyond right, a couple along the left and right field baselines beside the field, there's no way I can check them all. Even if I could that janitor probably left and won't be back until tomorrow. I'm opening the store with dad and he's going to wonder where I'm at. Even if I got here early, people have the entire rest of the day and night to see that telescope.

He's not in the building. He's not here. What am I going to do? This moment, this could possibly happen at the last possible time. In the worst possible place.

I just can't leave the equipment up there. What happens tomorrow when someone sees that telescope and investigates and sees my laptop there? It's locked but the telescope's pointed at the baseball field. They are going to tell the baseball team and they're going to realize what happened. Those people will tell on me immediately.

Can I climb the side of the building? I look out the window towards the grass edge of the building. Anything I can climb anywhere to get to that part of the roof? I am going to have to climb the side of this building. Three sides of the building can be seen by the field. The other one not. Not many people here. Just climb up and then I can unlock the door from the top. These buildings tend to allow someone to open a door from the roof to prevent people from being locked on the top. Climb up once and then get out the building.

I exit the building as I look for anything to pull myself up on. I see near the edge a drain pipe connected to a ledge and then another drain pipe. Go up ten feet shift three feet to the right go up twenty more feet get to the flat surface of the building hop the ten foot wall to the very top of the building to get the telescope.

I shouldn't do this. This is going to get me seriously hurt if I fall down. But I need to get to the top. My body isn't strong enough for this. My right arm is too crippled for this. I have to try. Pull on the drain pipe and it will hold my just under one hundred ten pound body. Right hand over left as I start to twist towards the left as I go up step by step. Feet against the wall as I start to go up.

Tilt heavily towards the left as my right arm burns. Pull my neck down and bite the end of my shirt as I go up towards the first transition. Three more feet before I have to go towards the right. Breathing getting heavy as I go up more.

Look to my right as I check the steel gutter. Dull not sharp won't cut my fingers. Thank goodness. Pull my body up then across towards the gutter my feet pressing now against a classroom window. Hope no one is there. Pant Pant. Step step as this gets more dangerous. Right arm gets jabbed by needles. Don't worry this is the last time you have to do anything. Don't give out now.

Hands reach the end of the gutter and my right grasps the bottom of the next pipe. Small creak on the pipe. Keep going quick. Left and right over each other as my feet get footing on the brick building. Crawl up more as my stomach starts to hurt and my feet don't want to stay on the building. Just pull as hard as I can. Pull myself up as I feel more pain in my right arm.

Left right as I spread out my feet wider on the climb. Deep breathing Deep breathing. Pull my self closer to the building. Sliding to the left as I hold on as hard as I can. Right arm back on. Getting to the lip. Right goes first then left as I roll myself on the top of the first part of the building. Sweat peeling down my body as I am safe on the building. I hear the announcer say it is now the top of the seventh inning. Have to get up and get the telescope and get back.

I roll myself over an air conditioning unit to the true top of the building and duck below the vantage point. Still catching my breath on each foot I cross. Having a person on top of the roof is suspicious everyone can see that. Disconnect wires while lying on my stomach. Disconnect and put everything inside the bag. Box this was on top of I can toss down I don't need to use it anymore, only a home game left.

Everything set in the bag just as I sneak towards the roof door. Clack clack won't budge it's locked from the top too. How am I going to get down from here?! I can't call for help that would be even more suspicious than asking to unlock the door. I am going to have to climb down. I vault back down to the second roof and look at the descent. Put my bag on the front of me. If I fall all the glass in there will cut me open if it's on my back. Though that probably will be the least of my worries. Box tossed down as it bounces on the grass maybe that could cushion a fall. Oh man here we go.

Hands grasp the ledge of the building right hand grabs the pipe and then the left. Straining on the pipe and my right arm. Go down and look down towards the gutter. Hands start to get moist and arms getting weak. Grab the end of the gutter and-

Ahhh!

My body slams against the end of the box and the ground. Thud as everything hits the ground. So much pain.

Am I paralyzed?! I wiggle my toes in my shoes, I wiggle my fingers. They can still move. Everything hurts. Brain still works don't have concussion. Can I get up? I slowly try to rise from falling down. I think the box broke my fall. I breathe deeply no ribs broken or lung punctured. I roll over onto my stomach and my back is in so much pain. Did I break my back?! Will I need surgery?

Slowly stand up as I start to limp towards the wall of the building. Is the telescope ok?! We need this for the final game. Air rushes back into my lungs as I collapse back down. My back hurts so much. I have to make it back to the game and the car.

I try and force my back up straight as I slowly go back towards the stands. The game is almost over and my body hurts. My arm couldn't hold me and my body is in so much pain.

Aaron's done his part that he needed. Now I need to do everything I can for him to get drafted. Be assertive for him. Defend him in public. Push through the pain for it. Use the money from the bonus for the surgery if I need it. I limp back towards the stands with the baseball in hand. This one I am personally keeping. All the hard work and pain for the homeruns I deserve at least one.

I take a knee right before I turn the corner of the field and wait for the game to end before I get back up. So much pain.

Chapter 24

Steph: Traffic Terrible Just pulled over will get back on in just a sec Tell mom will be at game as soon as I can :/

John: Game about to start will let mom know your missing the game

Steph: Your lucky I don't have more emoticons on my phone

John: :p

Stephanie will be missing the game, at least I don't have to save the seat for her anymore. I take my pawn bat off the seat. The top edge of the pawn glistens the sun right back at my face just as someone takes the seat next to me. Last game of high school for so many kids today. Even with Aaron we couldn't make playoffs. No banner this year but baseball is a team sport. Only one spot of nine in the lineup. If you don't want to deal with a hitter you can always walk him. Aaron was walked intentionally ten times this season.

Largest crowd to see the final game. No scouts, no college coaches, just fans and parents on the last day to watch. After this for most kids that's it for baseball. They go on with their lives beyond baseball. Baseball ending today for me one more time, and then that is it. No more helping Aaron, back to the shop this time with a little more money. Become Aaron's agent and that is wrapping up baseball. Last time to connect to the telescope.

Second row from the bottom as people came early to see the final pre-game warmups. Have my shoulders extra broad when I check the view. Still good even after fall damage. The grass in front of our house at that spot has a divot from placing a stand on the same spot for the past few months. Grass mowed in the infield and outfield just after it rained here yesterday. Moist with a few puddles just on the grass outside the field of play.

The varsity coaches from both of the teams walk out from the dugouts and talk to the umpires handing them the score cards, shake hands about to start. They say who the seniors are on the field. Away team's is their entire outfield and two of their pitching staff. Home team takes the field and Aaron takes his spot along the first baseline. Let's play.

One quick strikeout, bunt towards first Aaron cleats it and the kid takes first base with ease. Too bad they didn't have a designated hitter in this league then you could have sat on the bench for defense. Runner at first fastball low and away. Ball one. Manager at third taps his head then his right and left arms. Probably a steal maybe a hit and run. Pitchout signaled yup runner's going. Eric's covering base. Line drive back up the middle. Eric dives makes the catch. Runner gets up from the slide tries to turn around. Too slow with the run back. Time for the home team.

Randy up first base hit to the third base side. Sean up takes a walk. Aaron walks up to the plate with his bat on his shoulder soaking in the final moments. Pitcher's nervous. Everyone knows Aaron and what he can do. He can hit everything. Can't walk him will have bases loaded with the four five six guys up. Let's try the luck.

Sinker away. "Get a base knock now Aaron." Off the plate ball one. Sinker away again trying to maybe turn a double play. "Get a base knock now Aaron." Pitch delivered runners take their secondary. Boom! Ball going straight back to right center gap. Center fielder sprinting. Runners going. Ball going towards the wall not going out. Ball dying center fielder going fast as possible. Ball falling going to be a triple. Center dives into a puddle backwards and raises his glove in the air. Out.

Go back go back! Randy and Sean turn back towards second and first. Center fielder curl hops with all his might, jersey covered in mud. Cutoff second baseman lets the ball go. Sean rounds second. Ball bounces Randy dives back to second. Shortstop stretches. Out double play.

Crowd all excited for the amazing catch. Diving backwards and a double play. Just unlucky there. Still at least two more at bats. We got a good game coming up. Last time gotta get a homerun today. Make it homerun forty-three and break your own record.

Home team scores one. Inning over second inning. Away team scores right back. Home team up new pitcher maybe they went with an opener for this game. Seven eight nine go away hard. Diving plays by the infield, stretches by the first baseman. Next half inning they take the lead three one. Third inning top of the lineup here we go again.

Crowd excited for the chance to come back. The pitching senior rolls his shoulders about to start up what might be his last time pitching. Randy comes up fastball strike change-up ball. Glares at the third baseman playing on the lip of the grass. Curveball coming bunts towards the third baseline. Sprinting race. Randy top speed third base barehands throw stretch. Safe Safe Safe!

Sean comes up to the plate and glares at me. Should I help him out? No he wouldn't want me to. I look at my Mom and Dad. So invested in the game. The excitement. What's going to happen? That's why people love baseball. The close plays the athletic moves the power hits. Every play it can happen. Got to pay attention.

Strike one. Coach signals for a hit and run. Don't trust Aaron? Or are you worried about another double play coach? Randy takes a lead slow and steady, don't startle the pitcher. One look second look throws home. Clack as the slap sends the ball to the second base hole. First baseman dives barely has it. Sean sprinting towards first, no throw to second safe at second. First baseman chugs his body towards first leaps. Glove out. Safe says the first base umpire. Oh man that was close. We need instant replay here to check on those close calls.

Some people say that it desecrates the game to have video cameras checking on umpires mistakes but I ultimately think it helps. Since I used to pitch I remember how it felt for players to be called safe when they clearly were out. The extra burden it was to deal with that extra runner on base. More pitches to throw. Have to focus on the runner on base. Check runner have to still focus on the batter. Exhausting especially when you knew someone was out.

Aaron walks up to the plate. Ready to go again. Runner's same spot as they were last time. Righty with a curveball change-up fastball mix. Nothing special that we haven't had to deal with before. "Make some solid contact now." Strike one. Runners take their lead. Check the runner on second.

I faced so many hitters when I played. Faced so many pitchers at the end they started to blend together. But I know that Aaron has broken that mold. Everyone will remember this kid. Maybe not the name but they will remember what he did. What he looked like. The six four short brown haired superstar with biceps that could move a small mountain. Strong legs and hips to drive a baseball. Seeing everything with omnipresent ability.

"Wait for your pitch if you have to Aaron." The ball curves in towards him for a ball. One one. "Let's go Aaron." Ball just on the outside trying to get a strike but afraid if it actually is a strike and hittable. Each time I call out a pitch could be the last time I am doing it. Was that the last curveball I had to face? “Give it your best hack out there Aaron.” Ball two. Two balls one strike. Make this hit a good one. Catcher gives one finger down swings it towards Aaron and then lifts the ground. Last time he’s gonna see that. Too risky. Catcher up and the pitch fires. Aaron gets a piece of it right ahead of the fastball. Foul ball towards right field wind taking it out of play right fielder chasing.

Right fielder chasing. Sees the four foot fence. Ball going out of bounds. Gets to the fence ball coming down. Grabs the fence and leaps for the ball. The ball glances into his glove and his body falls over the fence. Does he still have it? Did he drop it? Raises his glove up. Yes he caught the ball! Throws over the fence to the second baseman as Sean stays at first and Randy goes to third. Crowd going crazy from the catch. He caught that ball.

That’s not fair. Aaron should have gotten another chance at it. That was out of bounds. The kid leaped over the fence. Aaron needs to get another hit another homer and RBI before he retires. Ok he still has one more at-bat left in the game for sure. Maybe two. But still that was not fair.

My mom shakes me, “that was an amazing play!”

“They stole it from Aaron.”

I take a step down from the bleachers and away from the game for just a moment. My back aching each step I take. He caught that ball. That could be the last time he has a chance for a hit. One for sure at-bat left. They might walk him. It’s not right it ends on that. No they won’t walk him.

Steph: Whats the score parked for a sec

Me: They just stole an at bat from Aaron

My shoulders tense. Have to refocus. Get that last homerun for Aaron just focus make sure every sign I send to Aaron is perfect. No mistakes. Only important person watching is me today. No scouts. No news crew just family and friends. That other team can’t take away this last game from me and Aaron. Cool off so you can focus. Back in pain but you have to pay attention. Just concentrate on the next at-bat and making sure the signs are right. If they switch pitchers figure the pitches and the signs from the camera. Done this before plenty of times and it will probably be the last time it will happen. Let's get that homerun. Time to win the last game of all time.

Runner's on third and first Eric up. Line drive in the left center gap. Rounds first one run scores. Ball coming in out a second base. Sean at third base 3-2. Aaron could have tied the game up. Every one gets stranded on base and the next inning begins. Top fourth one run scores 4-2 swap pitcher around on our side. Our ups again one runner stranded. Top fifth inning score held with their runner stranded after a triple. Our ups again fifth inning.

Bottom fifth warmups for the pitcher and a news crew arrives to catch the end of the game. Probably a news story for Aaron, but there is a chance they are just reporting the end of the high school baseball season. Setting up in the front of the visitor's dugout, getting last minute B-roll clips for the news.

Top of the lineup and they're rolling. Randy gets a double towards right. Sean up to bat, If Sean gets on base Aaron has a chance to take the lead and win the game. Squares for a sacrifice bunt. Third baseman charges. Pulls the bat right back and slaps it towards third base. Third baseman flails at the ball and it gets picked up by the shortstop runners at first and second one more time. Just take the lead now Aaron.

Curveball inside strike curveball outside ball. Slider away, "drive it the other way Aaron." Foul. Don't strikeout Aaron this could be your last at-bat of your career Aaron. Do not let it be a strikeout. Change inside almost clipped him. That would have been one weird way to end a career. Fastball outside up wants him to chase. Swing only if it's a strike. "Gotta take command out there Aaron." No swing for a full count.

Full count. Do not take a strikeout do not take a walk. Hit that ball Aaron. Most important at-bat in your career. The final at-bat. Do not let anyone wonder for the rest of your life what would have happened if you swung the bat. Make sure that your last at-bat ends in the best way possible. Crowd goes silent. Checks the runners. Pitch coming and Bang.

Yes! That ball is driven far toward left field, Left fielder chasing get out of here get out of here. Ball starting to die. Just make it over the fence. Outfielder running. At warning track. The ball is going to barely make it. Leaps at the wall. Ball connects with the glove above the fence. Body slams and creeks the fence. Flies straight down.

Left fielder gets up with all his remaining might and lurches the ball back. He caught the ball! He stole the homerun. Crowd cheering. Greatest play of the year they said. Camera crew catching the play. Outfielders going to check up on him. He stole Aaron's last homerun.

He's ok just as Aaron trots across the diamond back to the dugout. That probably was his last at-bat. His last career game and he went zero for three. Each one of his hits was stolen from him. He had the chance for a stellar game as usual but having it get stolen on each play. That's all of baseball and I just have to watch a game that I no longer have the influence I had.

Eric brings in a run but the rally gets stopped four to three. Maybe just maybe the chance for one more at-bat. Just one more at-bat. Need to get two baserunners on base. No runs on their end. Five six seven batters up for the sixth. Seventh inning away closer comes in for the last time and holds the score. We need two baserunners on base to get Aaron up.

Steph: Almost there

Lower end of the lineup usually the sophomores and freshman that made varsity. Time to shine you guys. Same pitcher, you've seen the senior for a few innings while he's thrown to the team. Make good contact get on base. Eighth batter grounds out to the pitcher. Easy out. That might be it. Number nine coming up fielders playing in. Smaller guy no power. Crackle. Ball grounded in the shortstop third base hole. Shortstop reaches got it sets. Sprinting to the base. Ball flies.

Safe. Still alive. Still one more chance. Top of the lineup coming we have a chance at this. Aaron has his chance still. Randy and Sean are too small to hit a homerun. At most they are tying the game together. Aaron can win this still.

Randy at bat. Crowd cheering excited close game coming down to the final moments. What everyone wants to see. Aaron just have your last win. You get to be the star. Coach gives hit and run signal. Risky risky double play can end this. Runner goes Randy taps the ball right where the second baseman was. Waved over to third base Right fielder checks runner and keeps it third and first.

Mound visit as the coach calls time trying to discuss what they are going to do with first and thirds. Let him go after him? Double play corners in? My sister's car turns the corner towards our house. Driveway blocked with other cars and she sees the cones in front of our house.

No! She is moving them. She is backing her car into the spot. Check the camera and the mini-vehicle is blocking the way. It's blocking the camera. No. No. He is about to go up with the most important at-bat of his life and it is going to be stopped.

Umpire says to get back to the dugout. Manager not listening. Umpire doesn't want to walk over there gives them more time. Stephanie walks towards the house and sees the telescope. She sees the screen of my computer and the car blocking. She hunches and squints. Umpire starting to walk towards the infielders and coach.

Stephanie dashes towards her car and moves it a few feet. Ok now I can see. She runs back to the telescope and sees the screen. I can see her mouth drop all the way over here. My phone rings in my pocket. Stephanie calling.

"Hello?" I ask.

"You're cheating!" Stephanie screams into the microphone. Quick need headphones. Gargle them in my pocket. "You're stealing the-" Connect connect.

"Um sorry we have bad connection," I mumble. "Talk to me when you get to the game please." Umpire walking back Sean starting to take steps towards the plate.

Stephanie runs towards her car and takes off towards the school parking lot. She's coming over here. I can't cheat anymore. Someone do something.

Sean at bat. Stephanie coming Aaron on deck. If it is a double play it is over. No first and third signs. I need to cheat and help Sean. Two fingers down wiggle away from Sean. "Let's Go Sean!" Come on you heard that one. You need to get on base. You know what pitch is coming. Jerks foward and takes the pitch. Calls time takes a few steps around the box. Doesn't want to cheat. Well I'm making you know what pitch is coming even if you don't want to. Looks at me and shakes his head. You're gonna know the pitch just swing and get a hit.

Fastball inside, "give it your best hack out there Sean." Runner checks Randy leaves on the green light. Sean lurches his body towards the pitch. Smack right in the ribs as he goes to the ground. He stepped into the pitch. He didn't want to cheat but couldn't stop me so he stepped into the pitch itself. Crawls himself towards first base as he rubs the inside of his ribs.

You can't be serious. Bases loaded. Aaron up to the plate. My sister has to be almost to the field by now. Last at-bat not a lot of time. Time to play for all the marbles. Everything ready. All in on Aaron Base to win this game.

The catcher stands up behind Aaron and sticks his left arm out. From the windup the pitch as they throw the first ball of an intentional walk.

They are going to walk him. He doesn't get a chance to hit. They are walking in a run and going to risk extra innings. They are taking his last at-bat away.

"Coward! Throw the ball to him." Ball goes back to the pitcher. Same process again as Aaron just stands there. "Give him the chance to win the game! Give him that last at-bat!" Ball two "Coward put me in there to strike him out. Give me that ball you coward I could pitch."

Umpire turns around and points at me, "He's ejected." The crowd and cameras turn towards me. I just got ejected for the first time in my career and I am not even on the roster. The umpire points his finger towards the parking lot and sends it flying. People are pointing at me to leave. Taunting the pitcher. They aren't going to start until I leave. I motion to my dad to make sure to pick up my Pawn bat as I turn towards the entrance of the school.

That was the last time of Aaron's career and he went zero for three with a walk. This is the last time I am taking this walk back towards the parking lot. Baseball field to the parking lot. Take a look at the school buildings as I go towards the main part of the school. Last time and it ended on a crazy moment. Stephanie passes the front gate and marches towards me.

From a short distance away, "John Base you just couldn't handle the last game could you. You had to cheat. You know how unfair that is to those people." Oh man here is Stephanie Base. Big Sister mad at me for misbehaving.

“You couldn’t just walk away from it all after last year. I’ve seen so many of your games I know what you were doing with sign stealing with that telescope of Dad’s.”

“Now sis you have to-” Oh no she realized the whole thing.

“He already had the perfect season, and you had to just rig the last game to be perfect. You couldn’t just cherish the good memories and let the last moment potentially be bad." She doesn’t realize this has been going on the whole season. She just thinks I cheated in this one game. One game cheating ok. She won’t tell anyone she will just get mad. “He was perfect and You had to taint it.” She gets out her phone I think she is going to tell mom.

I sigh, “well if it makes you feel any better. The good guys won and we didn’t get any hits today.” Just make her think it was today.

Closes her phone, “you better apologize to Aaron after the game. I know you dragged him into this, he’s too weak-willed to try anything like this,” she says as she goes to watch the ending of the game. Fine I’ll do it I tell her as she leaves but she only knows a part of this. Only one game that doesn’t even matter.

But it does matter, it matters to the kids that it is their last game. Knowing you can’t go any further means you have to give it all out on the field for the last time and if you still had stuff left in the tank it has nowhere to go. It has nowhere to go except staying inside you.

Steph: Going into extra innings Gonna be a while. Going back and forth

Have to wait by Steph’s car. if I go back towards my house right now with people watching someone might recognize me and get suspicious. That kid in the stands cheering for Aaron living right across the street. Can’t have math happen right now.

Steph: Aaron Struck out going into the tenth.

Those outfielders had the best play of the year tonight. Almost certainly of their careers. They beat me with their best baseball defense abilities. That will be the one thing in their career they remember. The best catch they ever made. Running full speed straight back diving almost against the fence. Falling over the fence to steal a foul ball. Actually stealing a homerun from a king. The pitcher actually can say that he struck out Aaron Base in his prime. The pitching staff can say they stopped Aaron

Base for an entire game. Taking his bat away even with all seeing eyes present. I got to witness the greatest game this season. I got ejected. I got memories that will last forever. This was my last game not one I pitched in but the one that I watched.

Steph: Thirteenth inning tied again for second time. Great game too bad you got ejected :p

Who won the game doesn't matter. It was exciting the best game even though we didn't get the best ending we got a great time playing. The excitement of each pitch. The smack of the ball that is what drove me to baseball and kissed me goodbye as it finished.

I start seeing some of the players walk back towards the parking lot. The game must be over, fans excited talking about plays in the game. Back and forth. It doesn't even matter who won. It was exciting the best game even though we didn't get the best ending we got a great time playing. That's what matters is the story not the ending.

I see Sean walk towards the parking lot. Season's over won't worry about Sean anymore, Season over. Baseball as I knew it is over. Now I have to make Aaron look like the best professional athlete. That is not just being a good player, but a good way to market product, the way how I finally make money off this amazing sport.

Chapter 25

Three Two quiet on set again. Three two one camera rolling. Action sign goes on. The studio band starts to play. Camera on the host in the green suit.

"Welcome ladies and gentlemen to another night in Charisma City. I'm your host Alexander Woodsman and this is Late Night with the Woodsman." Light for applause turns on as he gets out from behind his brown six drawer set desk. He waves at the studio audience as he walks towards the front of the stage. Points at one or two of them and thumbs up.

I don't know how people can stay up late to watch these shows. Filmed live at one in the morning. People should be sleeping at this time. Mom has work tomorrow so Dad came with us to the studio. This is so late, one basic rehearsal before this at ten o'clock. Different questions than tonight but basically the same. For Woodsman this is an opportunity to get someone on the rise on his show. For Aaron our goal this morning is to show that he is charismatic and can handle public scrutiny. Being a professional athlete, as much as I don't like to think about it is just as much being a public figure constantly staying in the public.

Band transitions from their brass instruments to the more electronic piano just as the end of the bridge to the song ends. Can't handle the public, you can't be out on a stadium. Can't be on a stage. A huge detriment to people is if they can't handle the public, if they can't, it limits the things they can actually do. That's why they pay celebrities so much money.

"Now people in Charisma City have been excited for graduations and the ending of the school year. Everyone except parents that are going to be having to watch their kids over the entire summer." Small chuckle from a few members from the audience. "Well I am certainly going to be having lots of fun with my kids over the summer. Anyone in the audience with kids?" Some hands get raised. "Tonight we have multiple guests on tonight and our first is one of the kids who just graduated. Taking with him the kitchen sink of high school baseball awards. Give a warm welcome to Charisma City High School's Greatest Former Hitter Aaron Base."

Aaron emerges from behind the curtain. His brown hair reflecting the studio lights. Edges of facial hair starting to emerge across his square jaw. Makeup artists just placed a little makeup on his forehead to deal with the lights. Make sure he is picture perfect and likable. The more positive attributes he gets the more likely they will offer more money because he makes them more.

Studio band stops their walk-on song, "now Aaron welcome to late night and let me ask first to our special first baseman, who you hoping to play for?" Woodsman asks as he takes a seat behind his desk and offers Aaron a spot on the faux couch seat.

Remember to promote your personal brand Aaron. You are a commodity now. Remember the talking points I gave you. You have to present yourself great. If people don't like you it's going to decrease your chances of a high draft pick. You were the high school league's MVP and broke nearly every high school record, but you still have to deal with other people. If stars on a good team don't like you they could use their pull with the general manager to, discourage, them from picking you. Either he goes or I go.

"Well I hope to get on a team that will go to the championship next year." Good Good. Aaron takes a deep breath, "better yet I hope to get on a team that I can carry to the championship next year." Massive clapping from the audience. Great job with that talking point. Multiple cheers from the audience and he isn't even playing baseball.

You have to present yourself as a marketable product. If you can get kids to the park to see you, you make more money because you have more value to the baseball team.

Feeding off the energy, Woodsman begins his questions, the audience quiets for a moment, "Aaron I'm sure that you will definitely do that. Though you couldn't lead your high school team to the playoffs this year alone. With a pitching staff like the Glove Poppers do you think you could bring a championship to Charisma City?"

A little concerned, "are you trying to get the Charisma City Glove Poppers to draft me?"

Show that you are cool under intense pressure. They might think that you can't handle stress and will crumble as a pro. Well, you are going to fall apart as a pro but not because you can't handle the pressure, it's because you're not actually good.

"As an unbiased late night host and a biased Charisma City resident and fan of the Glove Poppers baseball team, Yes." A few chuckles from the audience. Will this be good television? Don't know just get through this Aaron without hurting yourself and promote your brand.

"Onto my next question for you Aaron. You blew up on the radar this past year. No one saw you before last year. I actually saw your last game and saw your brother here in the studio audience get ejected. Granted you went zero for four on some amazing defensive plays, I have to ask, how did everyone miss you in your past seasons?"

Aaron stumbling, grasping at any words he can grab, "I honestly don't have any idea. I wish I knew myself."

Audience no sound. Woodsman squints. Tries to pick up after the bad question. Don't make anyone think about that Aaron. Woodsman taps the papers on his desk together as he looks at his script.

"Aaron you demolished a bunch of pitchers when you were at bat, to the point that some would intentionally walk you. Do you think that the pitchers in the league will give you the respect that you got in high school?"

Question that was on the prerehearsal good. Trying to make sure Aaron doesn't give a few word answers. Keep the guest calm and not scared most aren't actually used to something like this. They are on brand and only the host does this every day.

"Well my agent says that they better," claps from the audience. Ok good. "But seriously, though they probably are going to test me out on the first few games because, I don't want to jinx myself, but you know there are some players you know that just can't handle the transition to professional baseball."

Sensing the tradeoff of words Woodsman speaks, "oh I totally get it, when your about to hit superstardom sometimes you just end up getting hit. There was a guy who tried hosting a show and instead of being a host he ended up being toast." A little bit of audience interaction.

I guess you need to find a way to get everyone ready for the big let down. Getting all hyped up for something that turns out to be false would be so heartbreaking. You have to have them ready for what happens when you go and play in the league without me. Give them some explanation on why you can't play that doesn't involve cheating.

"Final question to you Aaron before we go to commercial, I noticed you had an interesting bat at the plate, and let's just say it noticed me back." Handoff to Aaron.

"Yeah I have a one of a kind piece of machinery that I use at the plate. It's called the ICU and I am the only one that gets to use it on my team."

"Ooo. The ICU only for you. Mind if I take a look at it?"

Why is the focus on the bat? Have the focus on Aaron. I guess that is at least taking the pressure off Aaron just a tad. We will have to find a way to get him to promote himself more. Going on a radio show maybe?

Aaron waves at me to grab the bat beside his bag. He's been carrying it since we left the photoshoot at the batting cage earlier today. Brought my Pawn bat in case he wanted to use it for the photoshoot said it was mine and didn't want to use it. No one ever sees the pawns.

Am I going to have to go on stage? They are waving me on. Oh no, my black hair is messy and my old baseball jacket needs to be washed. Jacket just slightly big for me even though it is a small. Stain just by the edge of my thin neck. Still waving have to get the bat.

Grab the bat and hand it to Aaron. Stay off the stage as long as possible. Should I wave. Back still hurts from the fall. Slow to walk.

"Ladies and Gentleman the guy who got banned from watching his former high school baseball team."

That's why he asked that question. He wanted me on stage just for that line. People are laughing at me. My ejection's going to be talked about by people.

"After being upset his brother was getting intentionally walked on what appeared to be his final high school at-bat, the guy you just saw started screaming at the pitcher and got ejected by the umpire. Gone. Not the ball but the fan." Laughter from the audience directed at me. "That was the first time I actually saw a fan leave near the end of a near tie ball game bases loaded. Before the play even happened." More laughter from the audience.

Woodsman is just mean. Camera pans to me as I don't know what to do. That bat was just the way to get me on stage. Now everyone is going to think of me as the guy ejected from the last game of the year. Ejected as the end to my high school baseball story and not striking the last guy out.

Camera goes back to Aaron and the bat, studio audience looks back towards Aaron. Ok that wasn't as bad as it could be. I got a scolding from my parents for my behavior and now local late night television mocked me. At least me being on the news won't happen again.

The studio lights make the bat look like it is glaring at me. Upset that I am taking my brother onto a TV show. Happy I got insulted on television. Upset that it is being used to commit fraud. But all it can do is see. It doesn't have a mouth to speak and tell everyone the truth. Omniscient but not omnipotent. Lacking the ability to use the knowledge it has, makes it like it doesn't even know it because it isn't using it. But some people out there do know what the bat knows. Sean, that girl, Aaron and my sister all are the other people that know the scheme.

"Nice, now I know if I ever need someone to keep an eye on the ball for me I'll call up this bat." Very few chuckles from the audience. That bit isn't working and he knows it's time to start to close up.

"Oh yeah, this bat has helped me throughout my career. Helped turn a few doubles into homeruns. Probably set a few distance records with this too. Has the perfect weight distribution for me as I racked up the homerun record." Aaron says just as Woodsman starts to shift his weight.

"With all the eyes on the bat how could you not see every pitch that was coming?"

Aaron goes white just for a brief moment. Oh no. No no. What if someone who can talk says what happens. Will Aaron tell the truth? Will whoever that was decide to say what she saw? Will Sean tell the coach? Will I be able to handle the pressure the rest of my life and not say what happened ever?

Woodsman doesn't notice Aaron being nervous, "last question is for the audience. Do you finally want to see one of Charisma City's own become the number one draft pick this year!?" Woodsman stands up and grabs Aaron by the hand and raises it up high. Cheering from the studio audience. Aaron trying to regain composure.

Music band starts to play just as the ICU bat wants to open its non-existent mouth to tell the truth.

Chapter 26

"As you can see on our left are the weight room facilities which have recently been upgraded to accommodate more athletes at a maximum capacity. And just behind that is the state of the art hydro-therapy pools for improving on muscle growth and strength development. As we continue through our new facility, I'd like to show you the hitter improvement center with advanced tracking technology," the athletic director says as he guides us through the University of Red Grove baseball facility.

I keep my camera on as we pass by the pitcher training area with different types of mounds. Nothing like my sporting goods store but still an excellent touch. Still live streaming our tour to ensure that every professional baseball team sees us doing a university visit. If they think that Aaron might walk away from a contract and go to college and play, then they are going to offer him way more money to ensure that he doesn't walk away at contract time.

The athletic director of this university himself is leading our tour. Usually, it is a fellow student or maybe for a better player a coach that leads the tour. This is the person in charge of all the athletics for the university. Most important player of all time has to be greeted by the most important person at the school. My parents are being guided by a dean to take a look around the dorms and stuff for Aaron. The stuff that parents care about at a university. I chose to stick with Aaron to record the livestream and not get bored with school stuff. They definitely want him to come here. He could singlehandedly bring millions of dollars and wins to the school. Who wouldn't want him at their school?

Catcher Sean: Saw Aaron on Woodsman's show this morning. Recorded it for myself two nights ago. He was bragging about how good he was. Disgusting and Shameful John. You climbed the side of a building to cheat.

I say into my phone camera, "we are about to go to another part of the facility, I just want to focus on that right now, the Bases will be back in a bit."

Look around no cameras at this spot close app. Open storage app. Select baseball video folders for this year. Video evidence has been erased. Video from the telescope that was on my phone eradicated. All that is left of that is memories. I kept them to show to Aaron if his swing was off but I never had to. Now all those baseball clips just gone, but they can't stick around. If I lost my phone and someone saw what was inside it, what would happen?

Open the picture app and force myself into a smile. Just remember all the things you did. Just remember them as long as you can. Can't go back to the video but would you even want to? Your greatest season but the secret on how you did it. Different settings, different backstops and different pitchers but the same truth. Countdown and smile.

I catch up to Aaron just as the athletic director shows him new baseball technology. Of course he has been focusing on Aaron ninety-eight percent of the time. I'm not the one coming over here. Showcase of the uniqueness of baseball tees, virtual bat tracking. Behind them is revolving pictures of former baseball athletes at the college.

Aaron interrupts the athletic director, "could we take a look at the science department's chemistry labs after this?"

The athletic director tilts his head, "the science laboratory? You wouldn't spend much time there, but just give me a sec to see if I can find someone who can show you that part of the campus."

The athletic director goes outside the batting area and into the hallway and calls on his phone.

I tap Aaron on the shoulder, his six four frame towers over me, "you know they don't want you to be in the science labs."

His head darts at me, "what do you mean John? This is a college tour."

"It's not really a college tour. It's a baseball tour." I brace Aaron for the truth, I am the big brother, I need to protect him, "this is going to sound so messed up, but they want you here to play baseball. They don't want you in those labs you want to see. Each day you're studying there is one less day you're training in this room."

"Why? They are a college," he asks.

"Are they really? I mean some schools sure, but a lot of schools like this." I wave my arms around the entire building. "Look at this school. Look at the other school we stopped at earlier. How much money did they spend on their sports facilities, not just baseball, but sports? Then think of how much they actually spend on their science labs, their university research? How much effort are they putting into their sports programs? Are they putting this much effort into their academic programs? I know I haven't gone to college and didn't have that much interest in school, but it doesn't seem like a college to me. It seems like a way for them not to pay you."

Aaron squares himself towards me "John they are giving me a scholarship if I go here. Money to go to school."

"They are just not charging you to go here. I guarantee you that they will put you into some academic program where you are in this facility for as long as possible and not taking any hard classes, any classes that you want to actually take. Classes that run into baseball game times, not gonna happen. And even if they let you take the classes you want, the moment your baseball ability goes away. Boom scholarship gone."

He points to the outside of the building onto the campus. "Baseball doesn't last forever. If I got a degree from here I can use this later in my life."

"Every employer is gonna know that degree from here is hardly a degree because you were an athlete. This program is literally not paying you to play for them. And guess what, you can't use your essence to make any money either or else you're off the team. I know, I'm your agent I looked it up. If you even showed an internet video of you playing and put an advertisement in front of it. You're off the team and not just this team but any team in this country." How can I explain this to him? I know how this system works. I studied it, I learned it for a brief moment in time. I thought about joining it just to be able to play baseball again.

Be firm John, "and guess what happens if you decide, Oh hey I'm just gonna be in the science lab doing science stuff all day. Your scholarship gone. They only care about your baseball ability, they don't care about your degree at all. And they are a school." I dart looking around to see if anyone is around, should I even say this now? "When they find out you can't even play. Your scholarship is gone too. And you are stuck having to pay for a degree that mom and dad can't pay for. You remember what happened when Steph got accepted to school?"

Aaron looks back into his mind, "I remember they were super happy when she opened that letter."

"And I remember later that night she got the letter, they were so upset they couldn't pay for it. That scholarship you'd get won't cover the science courses you want to take because it's a year by year scholarship. How do you think you're going to be able to pay to go here for an education that really is just unpaid baseball training in disguise." I point to the back of the room with revolving pictures, pictures of alumni athletes that succeeded. Pay us money and maybe you can be one of these people who play professionally too. All the money that you don't have. "They don't care about you Aaron."

"I don't think you do either John." That one really hurts Aaron. I've always looked out for you in the only ways I could. No matter what.

The athletic director's footsteps echo in the hall as he turns the corner back in. His portly weight, making the steps just a little louder.

"I couldn't find anyone to show you around the science labs. But I guess I could show you the building itself. Not sure how much good it will do though. I mean, you would be in here most of the time."

Aaron sighs, "it's ok let's just keep seeing the baseball stuff." I'm sorry Aaron. Your college dreams are not really college dreams. They are dreams masked in the cloak of the unpaid student-athlete. Not really a student, just an athlete getting ready to be a professional, if you even get chosen to be a professional. If you don't, then the only reason you are here is to get someone else ready to get on that professional stage.

Chapter 27

Catcher Sean: Turn on Charisma City news at the top of the hour you'll want to see the news about Aaron.

Strange, there wasn't supposed to be a news story about him today. Since I am legally his agent I've been making sure that every news article, photo shoot, and every social media post is controlled to improve his image. Show off skills, show off his personality, his bat even since he has been wanting that in his social media postings too.

Aaron on a video call with the Marine Bay Space Elevators at the table while I listen in behind the laptop. Asking him questions about all sorts of things. Some standard baseball questions about his abilities, others weirder. I think they are trying to get the answer to a different question than they are asking. You're gifted a one foot by one foot piece of land in the middle of nowhere what do you do with it? Maybe they want to see if you will invest in free team services but you have to work hard to gain the advantage of it. You have to consume at least five pounds of food a day for one week at what times do you eat it? What they really want to know is are you willing to find ways to reduce the time of required, but ultimately pointless, activities to get more important activities done. They want to see what you really think, not tell them what they think they want to hear.

Marine Bay Space Elevators have their general manager, manager, and batting coach on the video call as well asking questions. The Salmonberries actually had the owner on the call two hours ago. The Whitney Coast Cryptographers were basically letting him know he is going to be their first round pick if they actually get to him. They won the championship last year and are going last so it's highly unlikely that he is getting picked by them. At least we know there is a safety outlet for next week.

Please don't have a small market team pick him up. Small market teams are basically teams from smaller areas that don't have as much money as bigger teams. Smaller revenue less money for Aaron and me. If he does get picked up by a small market team maybe they would trade him for cash right after he gets drafted. Rich teams will pay more for the top talent, but he doesn't get the signing bonus from them.

I open a writing app on my phone. Type emergency message.

Demand that you will not get traded in contract signing.

IMPORTANT. Flip the phone over. Aaron says that he wants to be grounded in a place and not have to buy and then sell a house if he gets traded. Moon Crater's general manager gets nervous, they might not have the money to keep this person, good, they might pass over him for a bigger market team to pick him.

He needs to make it seem that he might not actually sign and go to college if the money isn't good enough and just wait. Wait one year and dominate in college and they lose their chance with next year's draft. Pay all the money you can to this person to get him while you can.

I open the internet app on my phone. I can't watch this on the television where my mom and dad can hear. Mom and Dad have been next to Aaron either on screen or off screen trying to give Aaron the advice they can. If this is bad news I don't want them to hear it. Where are my headphones? News is about to start. Slowly slide my chair away from the table and go towards my room. Dig through the stuff on my bed, not there behind the telescope? Where is it? I turn the volume up one. Rhythm of the news starts to go on. "This is Charisma City News at six." Found the headphones just by the edge of the closet. Plug in and go back keep one ear in the phone and the other out. Keep track of the meeting and the news.

Start to walk back to the kitchen, the announcer in her white cutoff dress stares straight into the camera as she reads the teleprompter, "our top story this evening concerns a major theft scheme." Oh man please don't have someone stealing from the store. "But not the theft scheme you would typically expect." I take my seat back at the table. "A sign stealing scheme." Wait I think I heard about this. That ice cream man had his signs stolen, is there a sign stealing ring going on in Charisma City?

"Baseball sign stealing. The process of getting a competitive advantage in baseball by decoding signals delivered by coaches and opposing players has gotten a lot more technologically advanced and even drastically unethical." My jaw drops at what I am hearing. Sean went to the news. He didn't tell the coach. He went to the news media. Everyone is going to know.

"Earlier this week we received allegations as well as video evidence which points to the existence of coordinated efforts to help promote the batting ability of Aaron Base. You might recall Aaron Base as the high school senior who broke the homerun, RBI, runs scored as well as the league batting average and slugging percentage by wide margins earlier this year. Well it appears that those records might just be tarnished." I plug both of the head phones in and dart my eyes to the phone. No one on the call knows what's going on.

"We have special coverage of a player on the team detailing elements of the scheme." Clips of the baseball games go on the screen. No No No. Sean's face right along side the baseball field, "I played with Aaron Base my entire time in high school and he wasn't good until his senior year. At first I thought he was just in a groove, then it was strange how well he was hitting. He was perfect. While I was catching I noticed a telescope like object in the outfield each game I was catching and then I started listening to the cheering from a fan." Back to the newsroom, "Charisma City news has reviewed footage of baseball games and at-bats of Aaron Base and have identified the voice of a fan who would say something innocuous but different depending on type and location of the pitch Aaron would receive. For example, each time a fastball was thrown on the lower outside part of home plate the voice would shout 'Make some solid contact'". Sean on the screen again this time taking a lead off first base. "To test my theory I listened to the voice. A change-up is a slower pitch so it would allow me to have more time to steal second. When he called for a change-up I knew I could take second base." Really Sean, you cheated too then, "the only way they could have known is if they used the device I saw in the outfield. It was aimed right at me when I was catching the whole season. That device is how Aaron Base hit so good. He knew every pitch."

"Our station has contacted the coach of the high school baseball team, opposing catchers to gather information and even pitchers as potential victims and we have not yet heard back. More on this story as we get news tonight at eleven." They didn't ask us for our opinion. Where is our side of the story? Granted most of that is true but they could have asked us to comment on it.

Interview on the other end of the table still going on normal. Stay calm. Don't make anyone nervous.

Please just stay local. Charisma City's media market is rather large but there is a lot of content out there. Maybe this will blow over and this won't be noticed by these teams. Buried in the news cycle and released to the public with no damage. If this stays in the area and is kept down, teams won't hear about it. If anyone who saw the news asks, just say what are you talking about. So long as this stays small this won't be a problem.

Chapter 28

"Aaron Base are you a cheater?" Push away a reporter.

"Aaron Base do you agree that you have tarnished baseball?" Make a space between the cameraman and the boom operator.

"John Base will you admit that voice in the video is yours?" Foreign correspondent with a thicker accent, this is international now.

"Aaron Base more evidence against you and your brother is mounting, do you accept responsibility?"

These reporters have been bugging us since we came over to this hotel. Baseball draft takes place in Marine Bay this year, and I thought this was a good time to finally see the ocean, but paparazzi followed me and my mom from the hotel to the beach and we had to drive right back. Aaron and my dad were actually bombarded as they took a tour of a science museum. We should have came the day of the draft instead of the day before.

Aaron grabs the rest of the luggage from the back of the car. The gasoline fumes from the multi-layered garage stink the entire building only ending at the entrance of the back of the hotel. Open the door for Aaron as Paparazzi are still snapping pictures. Aaron keeping his head down. Don't follow us in here, you're not guests.

The air conditioning of the building cleans the gasoline fumes and replaces it with fall air. Manicured walls and hallways before we get to the elevator. Aaron hands me a bag to hold and my right arm requests help from my left. Only fifty pounds but it still hurts after all this time.

"You sure messed up on this one," Aaron says. The talk of everyone who knows about baseball and sports, infused in most peoples minds. It's been on national news every day since that first news report. So soon before the draft, the best player cheating. A conspiracy. The ratings are breaking records faster than Aaron did. And everyone wants to talk about it.

I readjust myself, "Mom and Dad at least don't believe it yet."

The elevator door pings into the clean striped hallway. Hotel rooms for vacationing people intended to destress, but I am only stressed from all this. So close to getting the largest signing bonus ever given. There was talk of a baseline of paying him forty million dollars for a three year contract.

That probably won't happen. Slipping away from me. He might not get drafted because of the news. No money for what I did.

Hotel room 831 slide the keycard. Commemorative baseball draft room card. I will keep this. We go back to the hotel room to see my sister on the laptop talking to my parents. What she saw on the last game she kept to herself, but after her friends told her about the news story she had to tell the truth to my parents.

"So John's been the one doing it the whole time. Aaron was getting dragged along?"

"You sure about that?" Aaron looks at me as he starts putting down the rest of his luggage. Hello Steph. Good to see that you're tattling on me again.

"When I saw them when I parked the car I thought they were doing it for just one game. I wasn't paying attention and just thought John was just cheating so he would have his little last magical game. Then my friend showed me the news report about it and I remembered I saw the screen and saw John's computer screen and saw it all. I realized it was going the whole time. It's just no one noticed." Hello to you too Steph.

My mom turns to me and her eyes start to water. Please don't do that. "Everything you have done for the last months has been for this scheme of yours. Making us take two separate cars to away games, looking at your phone when Aaron was at the plate. Saying baseball things that didn't make sense. Running off right at the end of away games. The whole time you were cheating?"

I have to tell the truth, I motion towards the laptop and close it. This can't be on tape maybe I can salvage this. Sorry Steph, laptop shuts. "Yes the whole thing is true. Aaron never could play and he still can't if I'm not there. Aaron's a big guy if he could make contact he'd hit a homerun. He just couldn't make contact if he doesn't know what's going on. I used the telescope that I broke last year to steal the signs. That's why I never put it back on the shelf for a customer."

"You know how much trouble you're in John," my dad marches towards me. A lot I suspect. A lot more than I suspected. "You have gotten so many people in trouble. Those traffic cones you wanted, the telescope you used. They think both of us were involved in the scheme. A news report was showing our home. You know how much trouble you got your mother in at work."

"You need to go downstairs and tell the truth," my mom says as she sits down the couch inside the room. Hands in face as my dad goes to comfort her.

I respond frankly, "I'll get in more trouble if I tell the truth. Over time this will all blow away."

My dad speaks over my mom's shoulder, "Blow Away?! This is stuck on everyone's mind, legal repercussions and who knows what else is going to happen because of this. And Aaron still is eligible to be drafted. If he truly is that bad he shouldn't be here."

"He shouldn't have even made the varsity team. Honestly if I didn't help him you wouldn't have seen him on the field this year. But I can't take him out now even if I wanted to." Both are looking away from me. "What do you want me to do?"

"You can tell the truth," my dad says.

I can't tell the truth. Be strong. This was going to happen all along, we were going to steal from the professional baseball league. In this case everyone found out the day before. They would have probably have done an investigation because the superstar couldn't play well when he actually made it to the league. They almost certainly would have figured it out by then. Just deny like you were going to. Even if it hurts. You only have to do this for a little while. Even though it hurts so bad.

"I guess if Aaron wants to destroy his reputation he could go downstairs now and set up a conference. The only people that could prove it are me and Aaron. Or he could wait to see if he actually gets drafted. If he gets passed up because of the scheme then it won't matter past next week."

If we aren't drafted then none of this matters at all.

Chapter 29

The Spencestead Murkers are on the button. First round first pick someone pick Aaron. Please hold on to that same desire you had when Aaron appeared. Bell rings and they start the draft. The first few seconds pass and they go with Enrique Sansmar. Four Seventy Nine with sixteen homeruns. Ok first round first pick that's ok nothing to worry about. Getting the first pick is a big privilege and you can't risk anything with it. The Calcaptova Corner Painters second pick no luck. Ok don't worry we were the biggest fish this year but we only had a senior year. Sitting at the table in the conference room just waiting. Three more teams go by skipped over Aaron.

In less than a day the hotel ballroom was transformed to look like a sound stage. Controlled cameras to control the image for the television. All the fans want to know and see the reaction of the first and second rounders that get picked. As the draft goes on especially the sixth round onward less people will care and they probably will cut the feed to the other league drafts that are going to start soon.

Juggle around in my seat watching the big stage and screen other players getting called up ten teams so far no Aaron. More time goes by between the picks general mangers switching plans based on what has happened before. Who can they get, should they change strategy? Eleven more teams left for first round. Come on you have the greatest high school player of all time right in front of you pick him. The first first baseman of the night gets the first round fifteenth pick. They past over Aaron.

Three eighty-five batting average twelve homeruns. Just twelve homeruns over a guy who has more than forty. They are skipping over Aaron. The sixteenth pick also a first baseman. Not Aaron. The teams are skipping him over.

Take a sip of water at the table. Mom and Dad are here at the table all for ourselves in the middle of the ballroom. We were shifted from the front tables to the middle of the ballroom. Enough for the television camera to see us on a glance. Far enough away for us not to be important. They aren't going to pick us. Twentieth pick is a sidearm reliever as the draft goes into its second hour fifteen minute break.

Camera crew goes to his table as they see him and his family so happy he is going to be a professional baseball player.

I motion that I'm going to go back to the hotel room. Aaron wonders why I'm leaving. I'll watch the announcements there. Plug into the audio stream of the draft while we go back up. If they call our name, I'll rush back. Push my way back through the back set tables as I exit towards the main lobby of the hotel.

I got him all the way to the end of high school baseball. I got Aaron to be the greatest high school baseball player of all time. Every single time someone looks up high school baseball statistics they will remember Aaron Base. On top of a mountain, leaps ahead of everyone else, too far to catch records that will last until sports no longer exist and people no longer play any sport.

Open the door to the hotel room foldout couch were I was sleeping since last night. I take a seat and turn on the news, One ear hearing the baseball draft, both eyes watching something else. So close to it all and so very far away. Take a look at the mansion on the television. So close for Aaron to be buying that. I could have bought that car on the television with my share of his signing bonus.

The first round is over and Aaron got past over. The evidence is too great we're probably not going to get drafted. Whitney Coast Cryptographers passed us up. They will be back here any minute. They don't want to talk to me. Start to get the foldout bed ready. Say if I want any food from a sushi restaurant in the city. I don't want to go. Second round starts tomorrow at five P.M.

Still in my dress clothes from the draft I stare at the screen as a news report from Charisma City is talking about Aaron Base and reactions from victims of my scheme. Aaron Base this. John Base that. I close my eyes and don't hear my family come back in.

Switch out of the dress suit and into more relaxing clothes. Aaron going fully dressed to the draft downstairs sticking with a baseball pin that looks like his bat for the second round. He actually brought the bat with him in case a team wanted a photo shoot. I don't know if he would use it again. At least with it, I got the season of a lifetime.

I had fun doing this. I got to be a baseball player again and this time I was perfect. I couldn't pitch anymore, but I got to be a superstar that I never was before. A slugger who hit so many homeruns that eternity couldn't end this. A true king who saw all and brought fear to pitching staff to pitching staff.

Draft round two starting again. I don't need to go downstairs. Aaron Base, High School Superstar. Has a cool title for it. He will probably live his life out in a chemistry lab and science station. Aaron will probably be with me and my dad at the store before he takes off to science college next year when people forget and move on. I'll probably stick with the store for a while unless my parents don't want to deal with me because of this.

One hour goes by as other players soak up the spotlight. I soaked up that whole experience. High school baseball and a brief taste of the professional life. Superstardom just for a moment. The announcer on the screen wearing his bright blue suit walks back to the podium. "For the second round eighteenth pick of the professional baseball draft, the Steel Springs Moon Craters select Aaron Base."

Chapter 30

The mural of the Steel Springs Moon Craters decorates the outside of the hotel conference room as we wait to go for our turn at negotiating for the first contract. Signing bonus as large as possible, Aaron wants fewest years possible. Maybe if it's short he can later sign for way more money. It's almost as if the dozens of satellites of the Moon Craters logo are flying away from us. The single large observatory telescope on the moon of their logo looking up at the satellites or is it starting to look down? The last part of my baseball career is about to happen.

Second round eighteenth pick. Not bad. Could and should be better but at this point we will take it. The Moon Craters waited a round because they are concerned. After this Aaron leaves and I go back to the shop. No more baseball. He will do poorly without me, but I can't help him anymore. For a full year we saw everything on the field and reigned over baseball. The pawn dominated over kings.

Their first round pick comes out of the room and takes a picture with their negotiating staff. Two females three males, a large panel probably to grill him to take a lower amount. His agent sweating as he wipes his face and shakes the hand of his client. The team said that only a player and their agent can come inside this year. Typically every team lets anyone inside that meeting, family, media, occasional fan but only the minimum number of people this time, only for this team. I think it was meant for Aaron.

The woman in mint green waves us into the room just as the pictures are finished. I never really liked the Moon Craters mint green color for their uniforms, they should have gone with blue. Their tilted vertical checkerboard pattern of white linen squares by mint green squares all the way down the front and back of the jersey always seemed so weird, especially the two moon craters across the jersey. A clear expanse and calm moon surface with only satellites floating around.

The room, a modified hotel conference room, one that could be used for a small video session looks extra wide and empty with so much space between us and the olive walls.

They take their seats behind the broad wooden table. One of the men, late fifties, center of the group, looks at me and whispers to his colleague on his right.

"You know that I'm his agent. Supposed to be here. New generation coming in," I say to him.

He straightens his tie, and leans over the table from his seat, "we know that you cheated."

Aaron startled by him motions to speak, I put my hand in front of him. Time to be big brother. Even though Aaron is bigger than me, I'm still his big brother.

"Wow some pretty big accusations there." No response as they glare at me. All on the line, all the hits, homeruns and steals all for this moment. "If you think we cheated, then what are we even doing here and why did you even draft him?"

The woman on the corner in a white pantsuit looks towards the man at the center of the table, "we want you to come clean to the world."

Guy with the baseball cap, I think that is a scout that watched Aaron on the second to final game, points his finger at me, "we know that you cheated. You need to tell the truth to us about what you did."

They don't know we cheated. They don't know we cheated! Why else would they waste a draft pick spot that is worth millions of dollars. They want us to crack so they can save money if we did cheat and not offer to sign Aaron. But they are not sure if we did cheat. If we didn't cheat they are passing up on the best player in baseball history.

I need to tread this carefully, I can still get Aaron signed. Get Aaron signed. "Seems like a big master plan if you want us to come clean on cheating. Draft my client here in the second round. Drag us down here to a contract negotiation and say we need to tell the truth. No film crew or cameras. You could have saved a draft pick and just asked us in our room to hold a conference on cheating in baseball."

They don't know how to respond. I think that Aaron would have cracked and told what happened if I didn't step in. Please keep quiet Aaron, I can still do this. The news came out so late before the draft there is no way they could have seen all the video footage. Is there even video footage of every game to check?

"Look there are a variety of options here, option one we cheated and Aaron is terrible and you should definitely pass us up and we're scamming you. Option two we cheated and Aaron is somewhat good or at least good enough to be a professional baseball player maybe not enough to break even on what you will spend but enough to be an acceptable loss-"

"We think it's option one," the woman in the mint green says.

"Then kick us out don't give us an offer. Aaron goes to college plays baseball for a year. Reenters the draft. Still a superstar and then I guarantee you that he will be the first round draft pick. He will be out of your price range even if you trade for the first round pick. Or maybe he decides to go to a foreign league and you never see him again." Threaten to walk away. Only someone who is so sure of their abilities would walk away.

"Or I leave baseball altogether," Aaron says.

"Well that to," I brush my hair back. "I mean I wouldn't blame you after this past week of accusations basically saying you're too good to exist."

The silent one to the right of the head negotiator, "I think it could be option two." What is he going after? He turns towards his boss, "Aaron Base was phenomenal in his senior season. Did he cheat, yes he did. But what is his ability without the cheating. It has to be something." That something is nothing. He pauses for me to say something.

Don't admit cheating. Any mention of cheating ends this. The moment we admit to cheating we could even be banned from the sport. The high school baseball system banned both of us already because they believed we cheated and there is no longer a stake for them because we can't participate since we both graduated. The most important group is on the fence. Don't push yourself off.

The woman in the pantsuit goes after her coworker, "what are you even talking about? Look, him, these people are cheating us blind. He didn't even bat fifty in his junior year. We should have spend our second round pick on someone else and let this guy be a free agent."

I look back towards the head negotiator, "obviously if you don't give us an offer we can't sign anything. You have a few hours before Aaron becomes a free agent and a bidding war starts outside. You still have to deal with the fourth and fifth round picks today and tomorrow. What do you think is going through the heads of every other team out there? The moment we walk out of this room without an offer, we will disappear and you won't be able to sign us." Each one of those teams wanting to take a risk with Aaron is gonna want to sign him.

"Aaron Base, did you cheat?" the head negotiator demands.

I jump right in, "well you can't be going-"

"I want to hear it from him. You aren't exactly an unbiased agent here."

Aaron looks at me, and then right back at the negotiators, "I'm done here." He pushes his chair back and starts to walk out the room.

"Six million for three years. One point two million dollar signing bonus." The lead negotiator says and Aaron stops and goes back to the table. If Aaron signs after taxes that's roughly four hundred thousand in a bonus. Forty thousand to me. Aaron's money could pay off my parent's house. I could get a car.

Aaron closes his eyes about to make the biggest decision of his life, "six million dollars for the next three years of my life." Three years as a professional baseball player. Three of the best years of his life going to baseball for after taxes roughly three million dollars. A world of baseball that I won't see. But I guess it's ok that I don't see it. I got to be the best player when all my life I was just average. Aaron was the worst player but got the chance to be a superstar. Who could ask for any more than that?

Aaron nods and mouths ok.

"Sorry to insult you. We think it could be a third option. Option three where you didn't cheat and your former catcher is just upset and paranoid over cameras being all over the place. Part of option three is that the player that will turn around our franchise is sitting right across the table. This player will break every single record in the history of the sport."

Aaron blows air out of his mouth as the future has been set. Against everything that has happened this season, he is now a professional athlete. Something that so many people strive to be. Something that so many people beg to be.

"We'll send up a contract to your room to read in a little while. We had to make sure with these allegations going around about you." Shakes hands across the table and Aaron struggles to compose himself. Hands him a Steel Springs Moon Craters baseball cap that he puts on. Aaron shakes the last hand as he strides out the room and I follow him. The other people waiting for their contract negotiation to start.

Aaron doesn't look at me as we turn the corner past the other draftees in the hallway, "You ruined my life John. Took my college years from me. Those were going to be my best years John."

I try to deflect, "Aaron you could have said no." Bend around another corner as I struggle to keep up with his steps, each of his two steps is almost three of mine.

Aaron stops and turns right back at me. "How could I realistically say no to the contract? The only way that I could say no without being suspicious was by admitting that we cheated. All those events you made me do wouldn't make sense if I walked out the room and said okay bye. You heard mom and dad. They might get in trouble for what you did. I am the one who had to put up with this not you. I am the one who has to deal with the consequences, not you."

He yanks off his cap and blazons it in front of me, "this whole entire scheme and what happened doesn't just end right now. It ends for you when you're back at the shop while I'm in Steel Springs flailing at baseball. Guess what happens when the season starts? I am going to be ridiculed. My entire identity for the rest of my life is going to be based around baseball." He turns away from me as he keeps talking and keeps walking back towards the elevator to go back to our room.

"Not just now but way after they kick me off the team after my contract ends. Aaron Base, draft-bust, Aaron Base baseball cheater. Not Aaron Base the chemist. Aaron Base the science professor not gonna happen even if I spent my money on college, when people see me Aaron Base and hear my name they will think I am a cheater. Everything in my life will be baseball no matter what I do." We get to the elevator, press button no one inside. "They won't think of you at all. You hiding behind that telescope at our house in the background just a pawn in the system." Aaron press the button back to our floor as he leans up to the edge of elevator door away from me.

No press or media. Word is going to get out any second to the news about the signing. I don't care I need to tell Aaron this. This might be the last time. Aaron will have to go to Steel Springs very soon and he probably won't answer my calls.

"Aaron I know you hate me right now, but I really want to just thank you for giving me one last season to play." First floor second floor fast pace no stopping. "Look, I wasn't a great baseball player but with you out on the field and in the batter's box, I got one more chance to play. I got the season I couldn't have even dreamed of. I was there for every single homerun, every double, base hit, I felt that same exhilaration I had every moment you stepped up to the plate. Even when you didn't get a hit I was excited just seeing you out there. Me calling every single pitch out there and you getting a hit, I was right there with you. Memorizing every single code I yelled out to you. I was out on that field one last time." The door to our floor opens. No one in the hall. Parents still inside the room as they are starting to pack. I stop Aaron from going inside and close the door to keep talking, for maybe our last time.

"I'm ready to walk away from my baseball dream. You gave me something that so many people beg for and no one gets. One last chance out there. We always think it's going to last forever, but it just won't and by the time we realize it's over, we forgot to remember all the times we had with it. After the last play or just before does it hit you that it's ending. But you gave me one last time out there. So Aaron I know you might hate me and I totally get that. I really do. But thank you so much for giving me one more time out there. I savored every second we did this and if that is that, where I can't get that feeling of being on the field anymore, that's ok. I'll always remember the best season any high schooler ever had. You gave me the season where I got to be a superstar and everything that came with it."

Aaron doesn't want to look at me as he walks back into the room.

Chapter 31

The only noise for more than four hours has been the car engine and the occasional brush of air as another vehicle goes by. As we left the city between the fourth and fifth round picks, the radio injected more news about our cheating. After a name was called, our cheating would take the spot of the player's statistics, what their contract was, or their backstory. Only if something was more interesting than what we did was the only time they weren't talking about us.

Another burst of air from an oncoming car as we continue along the dark highway. My legs feel smushed behind Aaron's seat as my mom has started to stretch her legs over to my side of the car. She's been disappointed in me since I told her about the sign stealing. She got especially mad at me after she realized the traffic cones were being used to open up a viewing way. She hasn't spoken to me since.

Shining white lights approaching are now the brightest thing in the world as we approach the ramp back to Charisma City.

Aaron straightens himself forward and adjusts his seat. He hasn't wanted to speak to me much either especially after what was first something small, but then something a lot bigger than anyone expected. Why did Sean have to tell? He ruined everything. Since this all began Aaron and me have hardly spoken about anything other than baseball. Aaron adjust the dial towards some music to try and distract himself.

"Thanks Dan, the breaking news tonight comes regarding allegations of a sign stealing-" and it is off.

Aaron's body smashes the cushion back onto my legs as I keep feeling the pinch. My back still aches even as I sit in the car. Rolling onto the offramp as we get to the first red light.

"You're gonna have to pack for Steel Springs soon," my dad says just focusing on the road. That's the only thing to distract anyone from this.

"Yup," my brother responds not knowing what else to say. Is there even anything we could say about this?

"Planning on joining your brother over there?" my dad asks me. That's a huge question. What happens now? What do I do now with my life now that this is over? Being Aaron's agent won't have me doing much anymore except organizing the occasional publicity stunt for him.

"Only if he wants me to." I see Aaron glare at me through the wing mirror, he's done with the last few days that are just going to keep going on. "So probably not." He almost certainly won't want to speak to me again. So many people almost certainly don't want to see me again.

Looks like I'll be working at the shop for a while. It will be a while until I get part of Aaron's signing bonus. Maybe they might kick me out for what I've done. I hope not, but maybe I'll get a place nearby a professional baseball park. I'd be able to watch them play whenever I want to. Though I don't think Aaron would want for me to go to any of the games he plays in.

Green light, yellow light. Clear. Green light as we go by the grocery store. The empty streets where hopefully most people haven't heard what happened.

The last light before we get to our house and the only other vehicle on the street is a news van pulling up right beside us. Trying to be inconspicuous but the orange recording light out the side window is giving it away. It's either about the sign stealing scandal or it's about the signing of the contract. At this point no press is the press Aaron and I need. Maybe it's going somewhere else?

Green light and the van pulls behind us. It's not. It's going to follow us to our home and as soon as we get out of the car, they are going to bombard us with questions about what happened. Who was involved in the scheme? Who else knew? Why did you cheat? Three more turns before we turn the corner to our home.

"Do not talk to them, just go straight into the house and turn off the lights. Grab your bags from the trunk and go straight inside," my dad says. Anything we say about this is just going to be bad. The only good things I could say would be lies and those lies would just be to conceal and further hide truth that sometimes never comes out.

We pass the front of the high school where this all began and where it ended. Aaron Base the best high school senior baseball player in history. Hitting over seven forty-three with over forty-two homeruns to a has-been. After he graduates and maybe one year after he will be completely forgotten at the school. A brief historical note and maybe something to bring up at a dinner table all forgotten in a moment. Neither of us got a banner for the school for what we did.

Maybe if I helped the whole team we could have won one. No, that would have been too many people. Kids like Sean would have balked at the idea as soon as they heard it. But a whole team of cheaters. They would be unstoppable. They couldn't lose, and if the pitchers started cheating too put some pine tar on the fingers to make the ball more sticky, scuff the ball without an umpire knowing. They'd be close to throwing no hitters every day. They would be the best pitching staff in history. If you want to win you're gonna have to break the rules, just make it seem like you're playing honest and people won't know the difference.

Along the line of left field as we see a small group of people in front of our house. Are they fans? I think I recognize a few of them. Maybe this won't be too bad.

We get closer and I remember who a few of these people are. It's some of the pitchers that we faced and their parents. They must have found out where we lived from the news. About fifteen people in total are in the front area of our house, some on the lawn, others standing in the street waiting for us. I hear some of them shouting cheater and other insults at us.

I wish we had an automatic garage door so we didn't have to deal with them. But I guess no one expects a small angry mob to be waiting for them when they get home.

Some people surround the car as we slowly get up to the driveway. When you only see people in a certain way, in a baseball uniform then it's difficult to remember them when they aren't like that. News crew parks their van right where the cones used to be. The spot where I put the telescope has left a small mark on the grass from all the use.

The words from the small crowd go through the car window just as we park the car. Angry about what I did. Costed them a spot on the team, costed them a spot in the draft, costed them a scholarship opportunity, costed them so much that I don't even know. Hopes that Aaron's career doesn't go well. Blaming my parents for how they raised me.

Open the door. Aaron can you respond to the allegations against you? How could you John? Aaron is it true you're a fraud? Just grab the bags and bats and get in the house. You destroyed my life in baseball. Cheater. You don't realize how important this game is to people. I open the front door. Yes, I do realize how important baseball is. Close the front door.

I drop my bags by the front of the door and check to see if we left any blinds open. My mom puts her head in her hands as my dad tries to comfort her. I should say something, but anything I say is going to make this way worse. I walk towards my room as Aaron shuts the door to his.

Baseball is officially over for me. No more helping Aaron, I can't help him anymore. No more playing, my arm says no, years of pitching trying to keep up with bigger kids completely hurt my arm. I take one long look at the baseball pictures that are on the wall outside my room. Aaron always in the back, me always in the front, arranged shortest in front tallest in back. Part of Aaron's shadow always going over a bit of my shoulder, a bit of the cap in each and every picture. No more.

I open the door to my room and the stale air of the last few days whirls out of the room. I sold a lot of my baseball stuff to buy the bat for Aaron and me but it was worth it. I got to play one more season, the best season any player has ever had. Once I get my share of Aaron's money for acting as his agent, I can buy back all my baseball stuff and more. Maybe I can pay for therapy on my back from the fall I had earlier, it's getting better but still just slightly hurts. I slowly recline onto my bed and stare at the infield painted ceiling. Emerald green with a mahogany brown for the dirt paths. The first ball we got from Aaron's homeruns sits right beside my bedside as I start to close my eyes to sleep.

The telescope that I used, now no longer going to be used for anything sits right at the edge of my bed staring at the wall with nothing to see.

Chapter 32

"As Aaron Base continues to struggle in professional training before the season begins it is becoming clear the allegations of sign stealing are true. John and Aaron Base conducted an elaborate sign stealing scheme that has rocked the sport of baseball. Using a simple telescope they were able to beat the Charisma City region's best pitchers, they caused untold damage to the sport." I press my head down against the glass counter. Only the ticking of the wall clock can be heard. Last week, I got served a lawsuit.

The male radio announcer takes over, "it is now clear that Aaron Base will be the biggest draft-bust of all time. Him and his brother. That was there plan all along.They were in negotiation for the biggest signing bonus possible. They are the Draft-Busts. They busted the entire baseball draft system. They suck but if they weren't tattled on, we would have never known what they were doing." It was from the parents of the fireballer we faced in the second game of the season. They said because of what I did their son did bad and couldn't get the scholarship he was hoping for. They want the money that there son could have gotten. I think other people are gonna sue as well.

"The local television news conducted an audio analysis revealing a potential systematic cheating pattern from the words that Aaron Base's brother John was saying. Following a simple pattern you could understand what pitch was coming. From video analysis you could see the device that was used. Currently there is an investigation if these actions were indeed sponsored by the Charisma City government itself as there appears to be Charisma City traffic cones assisting in the device's operation. The mayor is denying any involvement."

They sued my parents too. They're really worried about losing our house because of what I did. My mom might lose her job because of the cones I used. No one has come into the store for a while because they think my dad helped out with the telescope.

Ding Ding. Thank goodness a customer.

"Hello sir, how may I help you today?" Hopefully this will blow over after a few more weeks. I told my dad that almost three weeks ago, but eventually something is going to replace this and everyone will forget.

"John Base! You were the one who stole my ice cream signs." The white boat hat ice cream man barges into the store. The edges of his uniform tinted from sweat from the autumn heat.

"Ice cream signs? Huh?"

A few of the business card racks jangle as he walks towards the counter, "I heard on the news that you and your brother were behind some massive sign stealing scheme. I spent the last few months trying to get my signs from the neighboring business. Then I realized, they wouldn't have them." He postures over the stand, "You were the one who stole them."

"I didn't even- sign stealing doesn't work like that." Not this person again.

"This is all my customers are talking about. The radio even every day. I am tired of running around for my signs back."

"Sir, we gave you your signs months ago and even gave a replacement for free."

"I want my signs back or I'm calling the police." He places both of his hands on the counter.

I cannot believe this nonsense, "you want to take a look around the store for your signs? Go ahead. Check the back even. You won't find them. I didn't take your signs. Did you ever play baseball? Sign stealing is when you figure out the messages that the other team is giving to give yourself an advantage. Is the other guy gonna bunt? Play in. Is he gonna steal? Pitchout. I didn't take your physical signs."

"I lost so much money from my signs being stolen."

"I'm sorry but stealing is part of baseball. You steal signs and you steal bases. I didn't steal your signs, but I stole plenty of bases." I think I'm gonna lose a lot more money than you from sign stealing. Way more money.

"So you're admitting you're a thief," he says as I put my hands over my face.

Ding. Ding. Another person walks in. Looks like a delivery person. Don't know what good it will do, no customers, no manufacturing. Won't need those supplies.

"I wasn't expecting a delivery today," I say to the younger brown haired woman.

She places the box on the counter, "the shipment of electronic signaling buzzers that was requested are here a week ahead of schedule. Could you just sign this for me?"

"Electronic signaling buzzers, what are those?" I ask as the ice cream man starts to look around the store and wait for the delivery person to leave. Where have I seen her before?

"Oh these are new age messaging devices. No need for all the old school signal flags or even using your voice to get your message across. Wirelessly connect one buzzer to another or even your phone, and boom you can have multiple options. Push a button and it vibrates, another option and it rubbles, from pulsing to zapping at over six hundred and fifty feet. Step into the digital age of signaling." The seventeen year old thumbs up and strikes a pose like she's rehearsed this.

I open the box and see the small buzzers. These are simple but they have computer components inside them that help relay the buzz that someone needs. My dad finally is having our store go into the modern era.

"These are really tiny, how can these even work?"

"Oh just because there dinky doesn't mean that they aren't good. A lot of people don't feel comfortable seeing the buzzer." She breathes in through her teeth, "it is a new age product and you know some older people well, don't like the effects of new technology." She thinks that she is losing the delivery," but it is perfect for hiding under a shirt, under a jersey, inside a shoe, I even heard one person actually stitched it under their skin so no one would see."

"Under a jersey?" I ask.

"Yeah it's simple just put some tape or something and don't take it off until no one's around. It's so small no one will know. Our goal with this model is that no one else can even notice our buzzer. Rechargeable too. Each one lasts up to five hours."

I sign the paper as I look at the buzzers. I wonder how much we could sell these for? I look back towards the girl as she takes a look at the old telescopes that I almost broke many months ago.

I question her, "were you in the gym watching the playoff practice?"

"No, I don't think I was." Oh yes you were. I just can't prove it. No one can prove you're using a buzzer either if it's under your clothes. "But if

I was I've given up on basketball and I've gone into chess. These buzzers would work like a charm there. It's like someone else is telling you now what move to do." She starts to walk towards the exit, "but who knows, I think I can still win a few games, might go back into it. Who knows, depending on what happens you might just see me again," she's says as she walks out the door.

The music shifts away again to the sports announcers, "Aaron Base will be forever known as the draft-bust. John Base will be known as the draft-bust. I can't wait for them to be gone and forgotten." I think we might just become hall of famers. I think we might just become the greatest of all time. I press the buzzer and a rubble echos. Fastball. Adjust the setting to a jolt. Slider. Second buzzer maybe for location. Nothing for an outside pitch, maybe a quick rattle for inside.

"Comparing his statistical batting ability from his junior year to his senior year of high school it is clear that an unnatural boost promoted such a player." I turn off the radio.

I am not going to let my parents lose their house. That's all the talk on the news is. Allegations. They can't prove anything. How could they prove a buzzer? That lawsuit is gonna base the stuff he did in high school with how well he does professionally. Aaron's always done bad during practice. He shines in the spotlight when his brother's there.

"Sir you want any signs in the store? You can have them all, I got some more signs to steal," I say as I start to close up the cash register. I need to buy tickets for the entire season Aaron's playing at home right in center field. I'll probably have to use my portion of the signing bonus for a place in Steel Springs. Almost every single away stadium has seats to sit in behind the center field wall, maybe not directly in center, but somewhere where I can see the signs. A couple others don't have center field seating, but that won't stop me.

"I knew you stole my ice cream sign," he points and gasps as he takes a step back. He feels that he has stumbled on a conspiracy. What signs is he gonna take? Oh man there's so much I can do with this. Down in the count but I know what pitches are coming, they are not ready for this.

Binoculars! I need binoculars. I can't use the telescope anymore, I wouldn't be able to hide that in any stadium. I go around the counter and start brushing aside telescopes and monoculars on the shelves. But binoculars, plenty of people have those at stadiums, especially those that have bad seats not behind home plate.

"What happened to my signs?" he begs as I ignore him looking for all the things I need. I put the black binocular strap over my head. Adjustable zoom, depth of field small. This should be good enough for seeing the signs. Grab a few buzzers and drop them into my pocket. Aaron will have to learn the new signals, but I know he can do it. That's all he has to do to become a superstar.

Where's my bat? Where is it? I don't care what they say, I need to have that with me. It will remind everyone of who is there and when Aaron is going to arrive. The first fan there. Just waiting, watching. The Pawn bat goes first before the ICU bat shows up onto the field. Whatever move they make defensive shift, pitching change, the Pawn sees you doing it.

From underneath the counter sitting in the case the used and unused baseball bat is waiting for me. Inside the see-through case the Pawn is about to make history. There are more important things than closing the shop. The ice cream man tilts his head wondering what I am doing, not having a clue. None of them will as I go to the next part of the journey. Baseball isn't over just yet Aaron. Not by a long shot.

I trip over a telescope to start a new era of baseball as I run out of the store, the new era of John and Aaron Base, the draft-busts and soon to be the greatest of all time.

To be continued.

About Jaime

Jaime Guzman has 15 years of baseball experience, and has played every position on the baseball field, though his experience is mainly in pitching, centerfield and first base. He also has immense knowledge of most other sports such as Football, Softball, Basketball and Track. Though he has since swapped his baseball glove for a writing pen, he still maintains a deep understanding of the sport.

Stay tuned for more stories by Jaime. I have a lot more ready to come out.

Get ready for the sequel to The Draft-Busts

The Hall of Famers

Coming Soon

Acknowledgements

I would like to thank my parents for taking the time to read this book before it was published. I would especially like to thank both of them for reading and helping me edit this book. Without their help this book couldn't have been made. There actions of taking me to my baseball games, watching me play baseball when I played allowed me to develop an understanding of Baseball that helped me create the story of the Draft-Busts into one that is truly believable to readers of all ages.

I would lastly like to thank all the boys and girls that I played Baseball with throughout my baseball career. Without you and the games we played, this book couldn't have existed. It was fun playing Baseball with you, thanks for all the hits strikeouts and homeruns that happened while we played. Even if they were against me.

www.ingramcontent.com/pod-product-compliance
Lightning Source LLC
LaVergne TN
LVHW051002080826
845145LV00009B/2406

* 9 7 8 1 7 3 6 7 5 0 6 1 2 *